WICHITA DÉJÀ VU

WICHITA DETECTIVE
BOOK SIX

PATRICK ANDREWS

ROUGH
EDGES
PRESS

Wichita Déjà Vu
Paperback Edition
Copyright © 2022 Patrick Andrews

Rough Edges Press
An Imprint of Wolfpack Publishing
9850 S. Maryland Parkway, Suite A-5 #323
Las Vegas, Nevada 89183

roughedgespress.com

Paperback ISBN 978-1-68549-197-0
eBook ISBN 978-1-68549-196-3
LCCN 2022948218

Dedicated to
The old Canal that flowed a very long time ago.

WICHITA DÉJÀ VU

"What the hell is déjà vu?"

– Dwayne Wheeler Private Detective

CHAPTER 1

Dwayne and Donna Sue Wheeler decided to buy their apartment. They liked the location on Market Street a few blocks from Douglas Avenue. The deal was made and Dwayne took some money out of their doorjamb to put a large down payment on the deal. They also got a permanent place to park their Nash station wagon in the E.Z. Parking Garage.

However, the business of Dwayne and Donna Sue's private detective agency seemed to be dried up. Each morning the telephone call Donna Sue made to Millie at the Reliable Answering Service was negative.

After noting it was two weeks of no capers, she hung up the phone in the outer office and walked back to see Dwayne in his part of the building.

"Dwayne, I'm getting worried."

Dwayne was optimistic. "Something's going to happen any day now. And, anyhow, we have a lot of money stashed in that doorjamb."

"I know, sweetie," she said. "We started out with the fifty thousand dollars you were given for those works of art you returned. But we took quite a chunk out of it in setting up this office as well as buying the apartment."

"I tell you what," Dwayne said. "Instead of calling the answering service, I'll check in with some of the outfits that have given me a lot of work in the past."

"Okay."

"I'm going to start with Harry Philbin of the good ol' Kansas Bureau of Investigation." He turned to the Rolodex on his desk to look up Philbin's number.

He dialed the phone and a familiar voice answered. "Hello."

"Hi, Harry. It's me, Dwayne Wheeler. How's things with you?"

"I have no problems. What's with you?"

"I'm interested in getting some work with you guys. Anything going on?"

"We have a lot going, Dwayne, but a new regulation forbids using outside aid. Thus, we won't be looking for any help."

"What brought that about?"

"We are now at full capacity when it comes to agents. So there's no reason to hire outside people."

"Well, thanks anyhow." Dwayne hung up and looked over at Donna Sue. "It seems the K.B.I. has no use for private detectives."

"That's weird," Donna Sue said.

Once more Dwayne turned to the Rolodex. He dialed Lieutenant Ben Forester of the Wichita Police Homicide Squad. An impatient voice answered. "Hello, homicide."

"Hi, Ben. It's me, Dwayne."

"What can I do for you, Dwayne?" he asked.

"I'm offering myself as a helper to you cops."

"We're busy but have a lot of new rookie guys going through our academy. They're young and eager."

"Okay. You won't be needing shamuses, right?"

"Right, Dwayne." He hung up.

Donna Sue could see what happened. "No, huh?"

Dwayne smirked. "I'm gonna have to go up higher. Such as the Federal Bureau of Investigation. J. Edgar Hoover's boys. The big guys, y'know? So here I go to do Agent Terry McCarthy a good favor."

The call to the F.B.I. was also futile.

Dwayne had a determined look on his face. This time he contacted Captain George Madison of the Kansas Highway Patrol. It was the same. Their ranks were full from having a large amount of new patrolmen.

Donna Sue said, "Y'know something, Dwayne. I believe I've figured all this out. All the guys who served in the war have been discharged. The ones that are interested in police work would have filled out the vacancies in law enforcement."

"Okay! Okay! So I got a discharge of Convenience to the Government because of my black market activities in Germany. That means if I want to work as a lawman I'm out of luck. So the best I can do is to be a shamus."

Donna Sue picked up the phone. "I think I'll call Millie at Reliable Answering Service again."

———

It was Dwayne's habit to get a haircut every third week at the OK Barbershop downtown. Donna Sue always went with him to go across the street and visit the Jayhawker Restaurant. This "restaurant" was really a diner.

Donna Sue used to work behind the counter at the eatery and she liked visiting old friends there. She was happy drinking coffee and dunking donuts along with her waitress friend Maisie Burnett. There was also Arnie Carson, the cook, and Slim the dishwasher. The place was also where Dwayne and Donna Sue had met.

Dwayne's habit was to leave Donna Sue in the restaurant and enter the barbershop. The place had plate glass windows on both sides of the front door, displaying the name of the establishment in gaudy letters of red and blue. The building boasted six barber chairs. Waiting customers shared a long wooden bench with a large coffee table holding magazines to their direct front.

Ernie Bascombe, the owner, was cutting the hair of one of the downtown businessmen. He looked up to see Dwayne walk in.

"Hey, Dwayne. How are things going with you?"

"Hi, Ernie. I'm doing fine." He saw that all the chairs were occupied. "I think I'll go to the back room and visit the guys there. Save me a place out here."

The back room was a working center for bookmakers earning their money through a trio of phones along the wall. They picked up the results from the various tracks around the country over a short-wave radio.

The gambling activity at the barbershop was an open secret in Wichita. The customers, mostly successful downtown businessmen, had prospered during the wartime economy. They went to the OK for haircuts because of its risqué reputation. The merchants got secret thrills from being in the company of "bad guys" putting down bets.

Most of the time it was the bookmakers who were able to grin happily at the results. The Wichita Police Department left the shop alone as long as the gambling did not become too apparent.

"Hey, guys," Dwayne greeted as he nodded to the trio of bookies.

They were Longshot Jackson, so called for his propensity of pushing horses with long odds on his customers. Ollie Krask was a corpulent man seated in a special reinforced chair that supported his huge body. He didn't give his patrons any advice. The bookie let them pick their own bets. The last but not least bookie was Rory Talbert. He was quiet and serious.

"Hey, Dwayne," Longshot said. "You wanna skim the *Racing Gazette*? There's some good horses today."

"Well, Longshot, I better not. If I lost any money on the ponies, Donna Sue would have a fit."

"Well, hell, you might hit it real big. You could buy Donna Sue a mink coat."

Dwayne shrugged. "Donna Sue is a serious Kansas gal."

"Ain't you ashamed, Dwayne!" Ollie said. "I can remember when you'd come in here and really play the ponies."

"Yeah, and I can remember when I'd have to sleep on the sofa for about six weeks when I lost all my money."

Rory broke into the conversations. "Y'know, guys, we should have a minute's silence to remember our dear friend Stubb Durham." He turned to Dwayne. "You solved his murder, didn't you Dwayne?"

"Yes, I did."

"He done more'n that," Krask stated. "He rid Wichita of them gangsters who came down from Kansas City."

Dwayne was getting embarrassed about the whole thing. He stood silent with the bookies for the sixty-seconds that Rory wanted. When the time was up, he said, "Well, guys, I figure there's a chair open for a haircut by now. See you later."

CHAPTER 2

Donna Sue was reading the *Ladies Home Journal* one afternoon when the phone rang in their office. She picked up the receiver and chanted her customary greetings. "Dwayne Wheeler Detective Agency. Where may I send your call?"

"Hi, Donna Sue. It's me, A.J. Kessler. Is Dwayne there?"

"Sure." She turned her head and called out, "Dwayne! A.J. wants to talk to you."

Dwayne picked up his phone. "Hey there, A.J. What's cooking?"

A.J. was a Wichita bondsman who was a little person, standing about four and a half feet tall. "I need you to go outta town with me to pick up a runner," the bondsman said. "It's Duke Cummings."

Dwayne was surprised. "He's been gone for a hell of a long time. Who turned him in?"

"That's what's so strange. He turned himself in."

"Well, he's not stupid," Dwayne said. "He's what you'd call a high-class embezzler. Where is he?"

"It's not close to Wichita, I'm afraid."

"I don't really care where he is," Dwayne said. "So I'll go along with you."

"Well, we got to go due north on U.S. 81 to McPherson," A.J. explained. "Then we turn west on State 96 to Ness City. From there we go south on U.S. Highway 283. We'll reach a small town of Waldo by 10 a.m. It's got a motor court. That's where we can pick him up."

"How far is all this?"

"I figure about 5 hours," A.J. said. "We can stop for breakfast in Ness City, then head for Waldo."

Dwayne was thoughtful. "We better leave Wichita around midnight. Right?"

"Yep. I'll pick you up at your apartment house."

"I'll be out there on the curb."

————

DWAYNE AND DONNA SUE STOOD WAITING FOR A.J. under a streetlight. They both knew A.J.'s Packard. The vehicle was designed to accommodate the little guy's physical requirements. He used a couple of sofa pillows on the seat. The rest of his instruments were a built-up accelerator, clutch and brake pedals. These enabled A.J. to drive safely and efficiently. He used a walking stick to reach the floor starter.

Another unusual feature of his automobile was the lack of handles on the inside of the rear doors. This arrangement had been installed to prevent passengers from being able to get out of the car by themselves. Most of these individuals were not voluntary riders; they were, in fact, prisoners of their diminutive driver. A.J. Kessler was a bail bondsman who went after runners with a vengeance. And when he caught one, he took him to the county jail in that atypical Packard as they sat fuming helplessly in the back seat, restrained by handcuffs and no door handles.

A.J. tooted his horn as he pulled up under the streetlight. Dwayne and Donna Sue gave each other a quick kiss. Donna Sue greeted A.J., then hurried to the door to the apartment house.

Dwayne slid into the Packard. "Ready to go to war?" he asked the little man.

"Naw. This is gonna be a piece of cake."

The pair, however, were ready for anything that might go wrong. A.J. packed a semi-automatic Beretta Model 1922, caliber nine-millimeter. This compact weapon fit A.J.'s small hand quite well. Additionally, he had a self-designed telescoping baton made of stainless steel. Its one-foot length could be doubled by the quick flick of a spring-loaded release button. The little man practiced constantly with the device, and could wield it fast and effectively against larger opponents.

Dwayne reached under his jacket and patted the .45 Colt semi-automatic pistol in his shoulder holster. They both settled down and chatted on various subjects as they rolled along through the Kansas night.

───────

THE DAWN WAS JUST BEGINNING TO CLIMB WHEN Dwayne and A.J. reached Ness City. A.J. spotted an open diner. "You hungry?"

"I could do with a breakfast," Dwayne said.

A.J. turned the Packard into the parking lot in front of the eatery. Dwayne looked at a petroleum truck parked outside. The pair got out and entered, noticing the two truckers who were eating.

The waitress was taken aback by the sight of A.J. Kessler as he and Dwayne sat down on a couple of stools. She set menus in front of them and stared at the little man.

"Coffee?" she asked.

"Yes," Dwayne said.

The woman cleared her throat. "Does your boy want the same?"

"Hey!" A.J. said. "I ain't his boy. I am a little man. And yeah. I'd like some coffee."

The truckers were also surprised, and looked down the counter but didn't say anything.

Dwayne spoke up. "I'd like a couple of eggs over easy with hashbrowns and bacon."

A.J. called for scrambled eggs, sausage, and hashbrowns.

The truckers finished their breakfast and got up to leave. They took quick glances at A.J. again as they passed him and went out to their truck.

The waitress stood behind the counter looking at A.J. "I'm sorry for what I said."

A.J. smiled. "That's alright. It happens a lot. Actually, my kind of folks are defined as dwarfs but we like to be called little people."

She smiled back and refilled his coffee cup. "I seen a lot of them in that *Wizard of Oz* movie."

A.J. chuckled. "I saw that with my wife. She's a little person, too."

The unseen cook back in the kitchen called out their servings. The waitress sat them in front of Dwayne and A.J. just as a trio of farmers came in. They didn't see A.J. but nodded a friendly greeting to Dwayne.

Dwayne and A.J. finished their breakfast in twenty minutes and slid off their stools. The farmers saw the little man as he and Dwayne left the diner. They had never seen a dwarf and were bewildered.

The pair got into the Packard. "Well now," A.J. said, "let's get down to that town of Waldo."

———

Dwayne spoke up. "There's that motor court."

There was a grocery across the street, but it hadn't been opened yet. A filling station, like a few houses, also weren't showing lights.

A.J. turned in to park in front of the office. "Let's see if Dukey boy is at home."

When they walked through the door they saw a man behind the counter and a suave individual at the front. He turned and grinned. "Hello there, A.J. It's good to see you." He noticed Dwayne. "Who's this with you?"

Dwayne answered, "I'm a private detective from Wichita."

Cummings laughed. "You're not the famous Dwayne Wheeler, are you?"

"Guilty as charged," Dwayne said.

Cummings turned to the man behind the counter. "I guess I'm all checked out, Ed. And thanks for buying that jalopy of mine."

Ed, the owner of the motor court, was pleased. "I like to meddle with old cars." He laughed. "Sometimes I even get one or two running."

"I wish you luck with mine," Cummings said. "Okay. I'll take these gentlemen down to my room so they can search what I got. Then it is Wichita here we come."

Dwayne and A.J. walked behind Cummings as he led them down the row of cabins. He laughed at them.

"Don't worry, you two aristocrats of the law, I'm not going to run away."

When they reached Cummings' lodge, it was evident that he wasn't going to hide anything. His clothing was spread across the bed and a sturdy suitcase was open and placed on the dressing table.

Dwayne and A.J. began to go through Cummings' belongings. Dwayne because of his larger hands patted down the empty suitcase while A.J. went through Cummings' toiletries. There were also two bottles of scotch. Dwayne sniffed them and found they were filled with legal whiskey.

"Save those bottles for the suitcase," Cummings said. "I can get them out for refreshments during the trip."

They took twenty minutes and when they finished, Cummings began packing everything away neat and simple. "Well, gentlemen, let us go to the wonderful city of Wichita," he said. "I can't wait to be in the confinements of Sedgwick County's jail."

"What made you want to turn in?" A.J. asked.

"Oh, hell, A.J. I was just tired of being a fugitive."

Dwayne and A.J. got in the front seat after Cummings pushed his suitcase in the back and sat down.

"Okay, Dwayne," A.J. said, "let's retrace our trip back to Wichita." He started the motor and drove back to the highway.

Fifteen minutes passed and Cummings had a suggestion. "Let me get one of these bottles of scotch and we can travel in style, right?" He opened the suitcase and shuffled around. "Stop this fucking car!"

"What for?" A.J. asked.

Dwayne turned around and saw that Cummings had a revolver in his hand. "He's got a gun, A.J.!"

"Okay!" A.J. said. "Okay!"

The little man pulled over and stopped. As soon as the car ceased moving, he and Dwayne jumped out. They pulled their own pistols and aimed them at Cummings through the windshield.

Cummings suddenly realized he didn't have any door handles. He started to shoot but both Dwayne and A.J. shot at him first. He was hit in the face by A.J. and the throat by Dwayne.

Dwayne opened the passenger side of the car. Cummings was slumped over, his skull split open with one eyeball popped out.

Dwayne noticed a concealed compartment in the suitcase. He looked closer and saw a small cardboard box that fell out. He picked it up and pulled off the lid. His eyes opened wide when he saw two one hundred-peso metal plates to print Argentine money. He quickly slid it under the passenger seat to hide it from A.J.

The little man pulled the driver's side door open and peered inside. "Goddamn it! There's blood all over the seat and floor! Well, he can't go back to Wichita. We have to stay here where the incident took place. The closest law is probably in Ness City."

They closed the doors and left Cummings where he was sprawled in the back.

CHAPTER 3

A.J. drove into Ness City and turned down Main Street past the diner. He pointed out the front window. "There's the courthouse, Dwayne. We'll prob'ly find the local sheriff there."

"Yeah," Dwayne said. "Wait! Look farther on. There's a Kansas Highway Patrol office."

The little man went another block and turned into a parking space. Dwayne quickly opened the door. "Wait a minute. I'm gonna get a pack of cigarettes."

A.J. jumped down, not aware of Dwayne pulling the counterfeit metal plates out from under the seat. Dwayne waved, "Lend me your keys so I can open the trunk."

"Catch!" A.J. said, tossing the keys over the top of the car.

The shamus got into his overnight bag and quickly stuck the plates inside before pulling out a pack of Lucky Strikes. "Okay. Let's go into the office."

When they entered the building, they saw a Lieutenant of the Highway Patrol seated behind a desk. The officer looked up. Then he saw A.J. and was surprised by the little man. He wondered what he had done to get in trouble.

"What can I do for you, guys?"

A.J. pulled out his bond warrant and handed it to him. "We killed that guy and he's in the back seat of the car out there."

Dwayne produced his private detective license. "I came along to help him."

The Lieutenant was serious when he said, "Show me the guy you killed."

They ushered the lawman out of the building and up to the back seat of A.J.'s Packard. "He contacted me from hereabouts and wanted to be taken back to Wichita to give himself up," A.J. explained

The Lieutenant let out a surprised whistle. "That guy's got his face pretty near shot off."

"Yeah," Dwayne said. "A.J. doesn't have door handles in the back of the car. That dead guy didn't notice it. So when he pulled his gun on us from the rear, we jumped out the front doors and he couldn't get out of the car. So we pumped two rounds into his head."

"Ruined his whole day, huh?" the Lieutenant said with a grin. "Well, let's go back inside and we can see my supervisor. He's in the back room."

The man led the two Wichitans through a small corridor to where the chief officer was seated at his desk doing some routine, boredom paperwork. He glanced up, glad for some interruption. Seeing a little man added to the pleasure.

"What's going on, Johnson?"

"This guy said he is a bondsman from Wichita. The other guy is a private detective. Both have got their credentials. They arrested a man who said he wanted to give himself up to the bondsman. It seems he wanted to kill these guys, but they got the best of him."

"Where is the victim?"

"He's in the car outside," Johnson said.

The supervisor stood up. "I'm Lieutenant Moore. So you're from Wichita, huh? Do either of you know Captain George Madison over there?"

"I know him," Dwayne said. "He's in charge of Patrol Troop F."

"Yeah, he's a good guy," Moore said.

When they got outside Moore peered into the Packard. "Yep. He's dead alright." He turned to Dwayne. "Now we don't have a..."

A.J. spoke up. "I'm the guy in charge."

"Sorry," Moore said, embarrassed. "At any rate we don't have a mortuary here for dead criminals. We use the funeral director when there's a corpse." He turned to the Lieutenant. "Johnson, give Lawrence a call to come over here to pick up a victim. And tell him the guy is a mess." He turned to Dwayne and A.J. "I'll drive you two over to the courthouse and you can speak with our district attorney. The sheriff will be interested in this situation as well."

Dwayne was impatient. "How long is that gonna take?"

"About two hours," Lieutenant Moore said. "Then you both will have to come back for the inquest. That'll be in a couple of weeks. Don't worry, the D.A. will give you all the information."

———

A.J. KESSLER DROPPED DWAYNE WHEELER OFF AT his apartment house at a little past ten o'clock p.m. The shamus wasted no time in hurrying into the building and getting up the stairs where he knew that Donna Sue would be waiting for him.

When he stuck his key in the lock, the door was pulled open by his wife. "Well!" she said. "How did everything go?"

Dwayne took off his jacket and unholstered the .45 automatic. "A.J. and I killed the guy."

Donna Sue stepped back with a frown. "What in the world happened?"

Dwayne explained picking up the lying runner, the lack of rear door handles, shooting the lying runner, going to the Kansas Highway Patrol and then the visit to the Ness County D.A.

"You guys were really busy!" Donna Sue exclaimed.

"We're going to have to go back for the inquest in a couple of weeks."

"Does that mean I can go with you?"

"Of course," Dwayne assured her. "You'll enjoy it. So will A.J.'s wife."

He got his overnight bag and set it on the coffee table. The shamus opened it and pulled out the small cardboard box. He showed her the two metal objects. "Look at these. What do you think they are?"

Donna Sue looked carefully and said, "There's a couple of backward-looking bills of some sort."

"These two objects make a hundred pesos of an Argentine bill. It's both sides when printed. These are used to produce money."

"What are you going to do with those things?"

He shook his head. "I'm gonna put these in the door-jamb with our other money. A.J. doesn't know I have 'em."

"Don't you feel like you're stealing from A.J.?"

"Hell no. He wouldn't be interested in them anyhow."

"Are you sure?" Donna Sue stated.

"Anyhow he was going to be busy having the back seat of his car changed because of the blood all over it."

"Ugh!"

"You can say that again."

"Ugh!"

CHAPTER 4

On the day of the inquest of Duke Cummings, Dwayne Wheeler and A.J. Kessler were seated at what was usually the defendant's table in the Ness County Courthouse. Donna Sue Wheeler and Irma Kessler were seated behind them. The courtroom was crowded and excited. Most of the women and girls thought A.J. and Irma were cute.

A very mannerly man sat in the back row of the chamber being as inconspicuous as possible. His name was Nigel Hawthorne and he was a stranger in Ness City. His driver, Herbert Rhodes, sat beside him.

However, the audience was more interested in what was going on in the front of the room. That was just fine with Hawthorne. If anybody heard him speak they would hear the accent of a most high-class British gentleman.

District Attorney Hiram Clinton was where the prosecutor usually sat. There were some items on a table sitting before the bench. The stenographer was at her place ready to start recording the proceedings.

The murmur died down as the bailiff stepped into the

room. "Hear ye, hear ye! All rise! The Ness County Court is now in session, the honorable Judge Tommy Fletcher presiding."

Judge Tommy Fletcher came in and took his seat.

The bailiff said, "Be seated. The inquest of one Duke Cummings, deceased, is called to order. A.J. Kessler may approach the bench."

A.J. stood up and walked over to the bailiff.

"Raise your right hand. Do you solemnly affirm that the testimony you are about to give will faithfully and truthfully conform to the facts and rules of the court?"

"Yes, sir."

"You may take a seat, Mister Kessler."

It took a bit of getting into the chair for the little man.

The D.A. Clinton walked up to A.J. "Are you acquainted with Duke Cummings, deceased?"

A.J. said, "Yes, sir."

"And what sort of acquaintance was it?"

"I shot him."

There was some chuckling among the spectators.

"Well," A.J. said, "Dwayne Wheeler also shot him."

Clinton remained unsmiling. "How did this shooting come about?"

"Well, sir, I'm a bondsman and Mister Cummings was one of my clients." He paused to take a breath. "He did not show up for his trial. Mister Cummings ran away and was gone for a long time."

"How long was he gone, Mister Kessler?"

"About a year."

"That is really quite a long time, isn't it, Mister Kessler?"

"It sure is," A.J said. "It's the longest of any runner I ever had."

"What is a runner?"

"That's a feller who runs from his bondsman," A.J. said. "But Cummings called me up long distance and told me he wanted to turn hisself in. He said I could pick him up at the motor court in Waldo, Kansas."

"And did you meet him at that motor court?"

"Yes, sir. I had Dwayne Wheeler, a private detective come with me."

"After you left the motor court with Duke Cummings what happened?

"Me and Dwayne was in the front seat of my Packard," A.J. said. "And Cummings was in the back with his suitcase. After a few minutes of going up the highway, he fooled around with his suitcase. Then he showed a revolver and told us to pull over." A.J. grinned. "Well, sir, there ain't any door handles in the back. Us bondmen do that so we can't get attacked from back there. I pulled over and both me and Dwayne jumped out of the front and turned and shot at the same time. The two bullets hit Cummings in the head and neck. He slumped down and started bleeding like a butchered hog. It really messed up my back seat. After we got back to Wichita, I had to get the whole rear of my Packard cleaned out and replaced with a new seat."

"What did you do before you drove back to Wichita?" Clinton asked.

"We drove up to Ness City and went inside the Kansas Highway Patrol office there and told them we killed a man that's sprawled in the back of my Packard. Lieutenant Johnson and Lieutenant Moore went outside and saw the dead Cummings. They took us over to the courthouse and we were questioned. They instructed us to return to Ness City for this inquest."

"Thank you, Mister Kessler. You may step down."

He slid carefully out of the chair.

Clinton turned to the bailiff. "Call Doctor Cal Turner."

The bailiff called out. "Doctor Calvin Turner approach the bench."

The doctor walked up.

"Raise your right hand. Do you solemnly affirm that the testimony you are about to give will faithfully and truthfully conform to the facts and rules of the court?"

"I do," the doctor said.

"Hello, Doctor Turner," Clinton said. "Did you examine the body of Duke Cummings?"

"I did."

"What were your findings, Doctor Turner?"

"There were two deadly wounds of bullets to the head. The lachrymal bone was shattered and the eyeball was blown away. The second wound was the maxilla that was crushed. Death was instant."

"Thank you, Doctor. What about any belongings?"

"All of it was soaked in blood," the doctor replied. "There were two bottles of scotch and some clothing in a suitcase."

"Thank you. You're dismissed."

Clinton turned to the judge. "It is my judgement that A.J. Kessler and Dwayne Wheeler shot in self-defense. There's nothing left in this case."

Judge Fletcher banged his gavel. "Court dismissed."

Nigel Hawthorne and his chauffeur walked rapidly out of the courthouse and got into a Cadillac. "Let's head out to Wichita."

The chauffeur quickly pulled away from the curb and headed for east State Highway 96. "Was there a metal plaque?"

"No," said Hawthorne. "But I am certain who has it. That would be Dwayne Wheeler. I know him quite well."

———

NIGEL HAWTHORNE HAD BEEN IN THE WAR WITH the Grenadier Guards of the British Army as a captain. At the end of the war, he stayed in Germany to serve as a liaison officer between the Brits and the Yanks. He was an excellent staff officer, but gambling, however, was his undoing. He got himself deep into debt to an illegal German casino in Frankfurt, Germany, Hawthorne fell into the classic trap where Communist agents set out to blackmail him into spying for them. They said he had better cooperate about his heavy gaming debts or they would be revealed to British Intelligence.

Hawthorne refused to be a turncoat. He knew he'd be the disgrace of his family if he were cashiered for conduct unbecoming an officer and gentleman, but he decided to take the only honorable way out. He wrote a note revealing his misdeeds along with an apology. He was cashiered in disgrace from his regiment and cut off by his wealthy father.

Hawthorne got a job as a merchant seaman. He worked his way across the Atlantic on the *HMS Elizabeth* and jumped ship to live in New York City. His suave ways allowed him to get good jobs and meet the right people. Hawthorne was surprised to see Peter Van Dyke, an American officer he had known in Germany. Rather than disappointment for the Englishman, Van Dyke invited him to join in special enterprises.

There was another man who was with them: Duke Cummings, who stole the two Argentine metal plaques.

CHAPTER 5

Donna Sue had just hung up with Millie of the Reliable Answering Service when a 1936 Cadillac pulled up at the agency door. She watched the driver get out and walk around to the other side. He opened the door and a man stepped out and looked around. He walked toward the door with the chauffeur following.

When the man stepped inside, Donna Sue was happy when she noticed he was an ornate gentleman. He said, "I would like to speak with Mister Dwayne Wheeler, if you please."

"Certainly, sir." She got up and walked through the door to Dwayne's desk. She spoke in a whisper, saying, "There's an extremely wealthy man out there in both speech and apparel. He looks and talks like an Englishman. And he's got a chauffeur."

Dwayne, grinning, rubbed his hands together and walked out to the lobby. He stopped short. "Nigel Hawthorne! This is an unexpected surprise!"

Hawthorne smiled. "I say, Dwayne, you do remember

me? And also those items you used to bring me in Chicago?"

"I sure do!"

"Well, Dwayne, I do believe you have something else to bring me."

"Really?"

"Yes. It is a set of Argentine metal plaques."

Dwayne was obviously surprised.

Hawthorne explained, "I was at the inquest yesterday in Ness City and there were no Argentine plaques within the dead man's belongings. He had stolen them from the U.S. Government."

"What the hell!" Dwayne stated.

Hawthorne smiled. "This is a legal situation. Another man is known to you."

"And who would that be?"

"Peter Van Dyke. And I would like to have those plaques back please."

"Okay, Nigel," Dwayne said. "They are back at our apartment. I can go get them right now if you want me to."

While this was going on, a 1940 Chevrolet sedan was stationed at the far end of the parking lot. There were two men who had been observing the Wheeler Detective Agency for an hour. They were known as Treasury Agent-1 and Treasury Agent-2. This was to keep them secret and anonymous. They had watched a Cadillac drive up and park in front of the detective's office. They noted two men getting out and entering the door. After a short time, they were surprised when Dwayne came out and got into his station wagon.

Twenty minutes passed and Dwayne returned and walked inside. "Here it is, safe and sound, Nigel."

Hawthorne opened the box and looked at the merchandise. "Okay, Dwayne. Thank you so much. You know, if you hadn't taken these precious items they would be in an evidence drawer somewhere. You actually did us a great favor."

"Have you seen Pete lately?"

"Of course."

"Give him my regards," Dwayne said.

"I certainly will, Dwayne."

He and his chauffeur left Dwayne's office, then quickly drove away.

"Maybe Dwayne Wheeler was hired for a case," Treasury Agent-2 remarked.

Treasury Agent-1 said, "Okay. Now let's get over there to see the Wheelers."

"Okay...whoops!" Treasury Agent-2 said, seeing Dwayne and Donna Sue leave the office. "There they go getting into that station wagon."

"No problem We can follow them to their home."

Treasury Agent-2 said, "Let's hope that's where they go."

The treasury duo followed them, keeping out of sight. Dwayne dropped Donna Sue off in front of the apartment building and continued over to the EZ Parking Garage. He parked in his private stall and took the short walk over to their abode.

The treasury guys watched until he entered the downstairs. They got out of the sedan and walked across the street. They already knew his apartment number from reading investigations about him. When they reached the apartment, Treasury Agent-1 knocked hard on the door.

Dwayne didn't like the summons. "What the hell can I do for you?"

Both agents showed their badges. Treasury Agent-1 said, "We'd like to talk with you."

Donna Sue was curious. "What's going on?"

"Your husband is under arrest," Treasury-2 said.

"What the hell is this all about?" Dwayne asked.

"You're charged with smuggling untaxed cigarettes, that's what this is all about."

"Are you talking about Pettibone?" Dwayne asked.

"We sure as hell are," Treasury-1 said.

Dwayne knew they had him high and dry. "Okay. But I only did it for minor things to get Ma Gilhooley and Shorty Barlow. And it worked. The Gilhooley bunch are in jail and Barlow is in prison for dealing in stolen cars"

"We know all that," Treasury-2 said. "And we could get you off free if you cooperate. As you know, Elmer Pettibone was the most powerful bootlegger in Wichita during Federal prohibition and the Kansas dry laws. He had a well-organized group of drivers who brought the booze into the state from a secret site. Now, of course, he's dealing with those untaxed cigarettes."

Treasury-1 added, "And you were one of those drivers, according to the law. We can charge you with making all those deliveries."

"But we won't if you help us with those untaxed cigarettes."

"What do you say?" Treasury-2 asked.

"What do I have to do?"

"Easy!" Treasury-1 said. "You go to work for Pettibone and find out where he ships the cigarettes from Wichita to the final destination."

"Damn! Pettibone is a longtime pal of mine."

"Okay then," Treasury-1 said, pulling handcuffs out of the leather case on his belt. "Stand up and put your hands behind your back."

Donna Sue shrieked. "*Dwaine Wheeler! Don't you do any such thing! You're gonna do what these guys want!*"

Dwayne looked from Donna Sue to the two Treasury agents. "When d'you guys want me to go over to Elmer's warehouse?"

CHAPTER 6

E lmer Pettibone was the proprietor of the small night club called the Roadhouse. It was expensive and only Wichita's social resister went there. He had also been the most powerful bootlegger in Wichita during Federal prohibition and the Kansas dry laws. He had a well-organized group of drivers who brought the booze into the state from a secret site during those exciting years. His best hauler was Dwayne Wheeler. The young man had a sixth sense when it came to avoiding revenuers' roadblocks and vehicles.

Elmer now had a different payload, and it was a much lighter one. The goods were untaxed cigarettes known as yellow labels.

After his conversation with Treasury Agent-1 and Treasury Agent-2, Dwayne Wheeler drove up to Elmer Pettibone's warehouse on Mosley Avenue north of Douglas. He was nervous as hell about getting Elmer and his drivers arrested. But if he didn't, he would surely get a five-to-ten-year sentence in the U.S. Penitentiary at Leavenworth. And there was Donna Sue to consider.

Dwayne parked by the entrance door and drew a deep breath before getting out of the Nash station wagon. He walked up and pushed the doorbell. He had to wait a few minutes for somebody to walk across the warehouse floor to answer the summons. The door opened and it was Jerry Owens, a driver.

"Hey!" he happily said. "Is that really you, Dwayne?"

"In the flesh," Dwayne said, forcing a grin. "I came to see Elmer."

"He'll be happy about that."

Dwayne noticed some of his old friends playing cards in a corner of the building. This was the veteran forklift team. They were two aged brothers named Harry and Dennis Walton who were bachelors driving for Elmer during the old days. Now they took care of loading and unloading the yellow label cigarettes.

Dwayne waved and called out, "Hey, guys!"

The two waved back as Jerry rejoined the game. Dwayne started to say something, then noticed a truck parked on the other side of the warehouse. This was something new. He gave it a quick look then walked over to Elmer's office and knocked on the door.

Elmer's raspy voice sounded out loudly. "C'mon in!"

Dwayne entered the door and Elmer's scowl melted into a happy expression at seeing his former driver. He stood up and leaned over his desk with his hand held out. "I'm mighty glad to see you, Dwayne. What's going on, good buddy?"

"I need a job," Dwayne said.

Elmer raised his eyebrows. "I knew you'd come back some day! And this is that day! By God this will give me two drivers."

"Well, you're right. The detective business ain't what it used to be."

"Neither is the dry laws. Running liquor is no more. And let me tell you the truth this cigarette hauling ain't much but it's all there is."

"Yeah," Dwayne said. "I remember the old days and the guys who used to do the liquor."

"You were the best, Dwayne. You was fifteen and sixteen, but you was the best. So now it's the untaxed yellow cigarettes game."

"Tell me the way that it's done."

"First off, the whole operation is the vehicles which are armored 1936 Chevrolet 1.5-ton trucks."

"I saw one of them parked across the back of the warehouse wall," Dwayne said.

"The high-up bosses of the racket made us get rid of all our trucks. They got new vehicles and had painters put phony *Hershey Bar*s advertisements on each side of the roadside sidewalls. They look like they're from candy stores."

"That was a good idea," Dwayne said.

"Each station only has to have one truck. Wichita is the fourth."

"But aren't the armored trucks kind of slow?"

"Oh, no. Now we can haul a few thousand cigarette cartons in the backs. The delivery is gonna be slow anyway because of traveling over bad roads. Just a minute." Elmer reached for the loudspeaker microphone and clicked on the switch. "Hey, Jerry! Get your ass in here!"

Jerry Owens came through the door after a minute. "Goddamn it, whattya want, Elmer?" He held out his cards. "This a full house if I ever saw one!"

Elmer snorted. "Stick them cards in your pocket and listen up. Dwayne is joining up with us so you won't have to drive alone anymore."

"Great!" Jerry Owens exclaimed. "I had a feeling he

was gonna hire on." He turned to Dwayne. "We get the run from Dallas up to here. Then we drive from Wichita to Kansas City. Did Elmer tell you about the armored trucks?"

"Yeah, he did," Dwayne said. "By the way is this Kansas City, Kansas or Kansas City, Missouri?"

"It's Kansas City, Missouri. Then we turn around and go back to Wichita to wait for another load."

"Of course each station keeps enough cigarettes to sell customers in its locality," Elmer said.

"Where is the starting point?" Dwayne asked

"Panama City, Florida," Jerry said.

"Yeah," Elmer answered. "They send the loads to New Orleans who drive it up to Dallas who send it to Wichita. The organization uses all the warehouses in crowded suburban areas. Like here."

"However," Jerry said, "we follow maps that give boondock routes through wide open country. That way we don't have to go through areas worrying about the law."

"Where does the Kansas City bunch send their load?" Dwayne asked.

"Chicago," Jerry said. "That's the last one."

"When is the next load from Wichita to Kansas City?"

"You and Jerry will start out at midnight day after tomorrow," Elmer told him. "So you won't have to wait long."

"Okay," Dwayne said. He looked at his watch. "Well, I gotta go pick up Donna Sue at her beauty treatment."

Jerry hurried back to the poker game and laid down his cards. "Ha! A full house! Kings over tens!"

"Ha!" Dennis Walton crowed. "Four jacks!"

"I'd be pissed off," Jerry said. "But I'm in a happy

mood since Dwayne and I are gonna be driving partners again."

———

DWAYNE GOT HOME AND HURRIED FROM THE EZ Parking Garage. He walked rapidly over to the apartment. "Donna Sue! We're gonna have to use the apartment and give up the office for a while."

"Why?"

"Just a minute," he said going over to the telephone and dialing.

Treasury-2 answered the call. "Yeah?"

"It's me," Dwayne said. "I got a driving job at the Pettibone outfit. My first trip will be with Jerry Owens at midnight day after tomorrow."

"Yeah," said Treasury-2. "Owens is on our list."

Treasury-1 broke in. "What's the complete route schedule for the whole operation?"

"Panama City, New Orleans, Dallas, Wichita, Kansas City then Chicago."

"Is that Kansas City, Kansas or Missouri."

"Missouri," Dwayne said. "Everything's the same except for the trucks."

"What kind are they?" Treasury-2 asked.

"All are 1936 1.5-ton Chevrolet trucks. And they are armored vehicles along with being camouflaged to look like they're hauling Hershey Bars."

"Interesting," Treasury-1 remarked. "We want you to spend as much time as possible in Pettibone's warehouse. Pick up any valuable information you can and call us when you get home in the evenings."

Treasury-2 added, "If there's anything really important, give us a call."

"As they say in the Army," Dwayne said, "Wilco. That's short for *will comply*."

"Right!" Treasury-1 acknowledged.

Dwayne hung up and turned to Donna Sue. "Let's go to the Stockyards Restaurant for some great steaks."

"Sounds good."

"And I'll tell you everything."

CHAPTER 7

The Dallas truck had arrived and the Walton brothers used the forklift to unload Wichita's yellow label cigarettes. With that done, they turned their attention to the Kansas City and Chicago shipments. The four pallets were fitted easily into the back of the Wichita truck.

The Texas drivers, not a talkative pair, wasted no time in heading back to Dallas.

———

DWAYNE HAD SLEPT THROUGH THE AFTERNOON and evening to be wakeful for his run to Kansas City. The trouble was that he kept waking up. Jerry Owens who had made a lot of runs would be getting hours of refreshing sleep.

Dwayne gave up trying to get any rest and he finally got out of bed and dressed. Donna Sue woke up. "I guess you're gonna run those cigarettes, huh? Don't forget your sandwich and coffee."

"I won't." He kissed her and took a change of clothing.

Dwayne went to the E.Z. Parking Garage and got into his station wagon. He drove over to Elmer's warehouse. Jerry Owens showed up ten minutes later and parked his Ford coupe next to Dwayne's vehicle. Dwayne was surprised to see him carrying an M1 rifle.

Jerry went over to fill the truck's tank with gasoline while Dwayne watched. As soon as Jerry finished his chore, he got into the cab and started the motor. Dwayne climbed into the armored truck and sat next to him.

Jerry glanced at Dwayne. "Ready to go?"

"I sure am. Just how far is it to Kansas City?"

"Close to two hunnerd miles," Jerry said. "That's as the birds fly but we can't do it that way. It's because we're gotta keep off the highways. We'll be zig-zagging along farm roads and through small towns. That's why it'll be more than twice that far."

"So how long does that take?"

"Something like twenty hours," Jerry said. "I think so, anyhow. My arithmetic ain't too good."

Fifteen minutes later, they crossed the city limits of Wichita and turned north.

———

"How about filling my thermos cup, Dwayne?" Jerry asked.

"You got it."

He unscrewed the lid and poured some coffee for his partner. Then he did the same for himself.

A couple of hours passed while Dwayne smoked Lucky Strikes and Jerry Chesterfield cigarettes. Dwayne peered through the front and side windows. It was dark most of the time, but now and then there would be a small town's streetlights as they rolled through a rural community.

Jerry looked at him. "You ain't sleepy, are you?"

"Nope. This is all too new to me to want to sleep."

"You want to drive now?

"Sure!"

Jerry stopped in the middle of the road and the pair changed places. He settled in the passenger seat and leaned back.

Dwayne, after he put the vehicle in gear, began having fun driving the 1.5-ton armored truck. At one time he was going along a dirt road and was surprised by jackrabbits running in the headlight illumination then suddenly veering away.

———

JERRY, WHO HAD BEEN DOZING, SAT STRAIGHT up. He looked over at Dwayne. "You want some java?"

"Sure."

Jerry served coffee for both of them, then settled back. "Say, Dwayne. Were you in the service during the war?"

"Yeah. I was in the military police in the E.T.O. What about you?"

"I was drafted into the 137th Infantry Regiment. We served in the E.T.O., too."

"Wow!" Dwayne said. "I see why you have that M1 rifle. Anyway, I enlisted before the war. When the real fighting started I got shipped to Europe to do M.P. duties. I just directed traffic and fooled around on the black market. I worked my way up to master sergeant."

"I made staff sergeant," Jerry said.

"I'm afraid to say it, but I got one of them Convenience of the Government Discharges."

"The black market must have been pretty tempting," Jerry said.

"I'll say. I was in it with my commanding officer but he didn't get caught."

A silence settled in for twenty minutes, then Jerry said. "I'll take over driving."

Dwayne braked and they got out to cross each other in front of the truck. When they were settled down, Jerry got the heavy vehicle rolling along.

———

Dwayne woke up when the sound of the engine eased off. He opened his eyes and saw they were in an industrial area.

"We're nearly there," Jerry said.

Now Dwayne could see it was early evening. He looked up and saw a DC3 airliner flying toward the Kansas City airport. A bad experience suddenly hit his memory. It had been when he was submerged in a gang war among Irish thugs, a Sicilian mob and two different Mafia families. It was during *Operation Undercover*. All this in the middle of the Kansas prairie.

A member of the Derby Gang by the name of Dennis Murphy had ratted out his mob. The Irish boss Johnny Cullen was called from Boston and informed what Murphy had done. He sent the guy flying out from Boston to get zapped. The reception committee would be an execution squad.

When Murphy showed up in the Kansas City airport, a welcoming group of four Irishmen met him. They were jovial and happy as they took Murphy across the Kansas line. After two hours, the driver suddenly turned into a grove of cottonwood trees and stopped. From the change of attitudes of the Irish gang Murphy now knew he was in his last minutes of life. His pleas for mercy ended when he got a bullet in the back of the head. Then the Irishmen dug a shallow grave in a copse and threw the dead man into the hole. After the dirt was thrown on him and stamped down, the death party went back to report to Johnny Cullen.

———————

DWAYNE SIGHED AND TURNED HIS THOUGHTS TO yellow label cigarettes going to Kansas City.

Jerry Owens drove through an opening in a wire fence and up to a large portal. He honked several times and the door was pushed open by a man inside. He gave a friendly wave as the truck was driven in.

"Hey, Jerry!"

Jerry and Dwayne got down from the cab and walked around to the front of the truck. "Hi, Darrell. This is Dwayne."

Darrell stuck out his hand with a smile. "Hey, Dwayne. Glad to know you."

"Same here," Dwayne said, shaking the offered gloved hand.

A forklift came up to the truck and Jerry turned the handle on the truck's rear gate and pushed it up. He and Dwayne watched the guy skillfully remove the Kansas City pallet and drive it over to a workbench. He went back to get the final load into the Chicago-bound truck.

Jerry was standing by Dwayne. "Well, we've done our job. There's a pretty good restaurant here."

"Is it like the Stockyard Restaurant in Wichita?"

Jerry shrugged. "They're about the same. And there's a motor court where you can sleep and rest up and change clothes. Unless you want to nap in the warehouse."

"I'll take the motor court, thank you," Dwayne said.

———

AFTER THE RETURN OF THE TRUCK TO WICHITA arrived, Dwayne got into his station wagon and drove to the parking lot. As usual he walked to the apartment house and gave Donna Sue a sexy kiss.

Donna Sue smiled. "Now don't tell me you're horny."

"You bet, but I got to contact the treasury connections before there's any fun stuff." He dialed the number and Treasury-1 answered. Dwayne spoke up. "I'm back from the first run."

"How was it?"

"Bumpy and slow. But we got the Kansas City stuff dropped off and put the cigarettes on the Chicago truck that was waiting for their load."

"So everything is up-to-date and okay?"

"Yeah."

Dwayne hung up and looked over at Donna Sue. "Would you believe I'm not horny?"

"You're tired, honey," Donna Sue said. "You'll get use to the hours."

CHAPTER 8

Out in a desolate area of western Kansas was a building that served as a training school for code-breakers during World War II. It was a medium sized fortress with cement blocks stacked around it as a twelve-foot-high endless bastion. The size of the three story building was 50 yards on all four sides.

The students were male and female with the females being the smarter cryptographers when it came to learning sending and receiving coded messages. However, the instructors were all men.

At the end of the war the training was brought to a halt. The building had been wired for batteries to drive the water pump and lights for the three floors, restrooms and showers. Every piece of furniture, kitchenware, radios, airport equipment had been taken out and shipped to a U.S. supply warehouse in Nevada.

When the Japanese surrendered, all assigned personnel were discharged and transferred back to civilian life. With that done, the entire garrison was completely forgotten by the Federal government.

After two years it was opened to conduct a South American program. The nations of Argentina, Bolivia, Chile, Paraguay and Uruguay were having trouble with forgery from secret Nazi sources in spite of the end of the European campaigns.

A special team of remarkable people moved into the codebreaker building to begin ending the crimes.

An inspection was carried on by Nigel Hawthorne and Herbert Rhone. The two found that the building was no longer a tranquil place but could be cleaned up and comfortable. Herbert Rhone took some photos while Hawthorne went from the basement to the top of the building.

After Hawthorne and Rhodes returned to Washington, they made a long distance phone call and reported to their leader. The man was pleased. All the equipment, tools and accessories to begin their work was in a storage facility ready to pack up.

———

Dwayne had taken a half dozen deliveries to Kansas City and he and Jerry Owens were building a friendship. Jerry's wife Melanie and Donna Sue hit it off right away, too. The two couples liked going to the Stockyards Restaurant, movies and the Riverside Park on Sundays.

One night, after seeing the movie *Meet Me in Saint Louis* at the Miller Theater, they went to the Armstrong Finer Ice Cream Store.

"That little Judy Garland is such a wonderful singer," Donna Sue commented.

"Yeah," Jerry said. "I liked the news reels and cartoons, too."

"Next week we'll see Robert Mitchum at the Orpheum," Dwayne said. "It's *Out of the Past.*"

After getting stuffed on ice cream, Dwayne drove the Owens to their house then headed for the EZ Parking Garage. They wasted no time to start preparing for bed.

Donna Sue began taking off her makeup while Dwayne, already in his pajamas, went into the bathroom to brush his teeth, then came out. He stretched and yawned, and settled under the covers.

Donna Sue got into bed and snuggled down. It wasn't long before she was sleeping soundly and Dwayne was wide awake. His mind soon bothered him as he knew he was doing something that would be going bad for Jerry, Elmer and the Walton brothers. The Treasures-1 and -2 were sure to get Elmer into the penitentiary for a long time.

He remembered A.J. and him killing that son of a bitch Duke Cummings. Donna Sue considered both him and A.J. doing the right thing by the act. But there was two times in the past Dwayne had taken other men's lives. And he'd never told Donna Sue about it.

This was another episode in *Operation Undercover* he remembered.

The Forzini Mob, Banocci Crime family, the Derby Gang and the Lunari Gang in Boston were the bad guys. Dwayne was in deep cover with F.B.I. agent Terry McCarthy. The shamus, Terry, and Frank Quinn ended up getting orders from Johnny Cullen, the boss of the Derby Gang. Dwayne was to kill Fat Pauly Cappurio of the Forzini Mob. It was to be done in the dark among parked eight-wheelers at a truck stop.

Dwayne and his two companions hurried down to the trucks. They reached a handy spot and stepped back into the darkness between two of the rigs. Dwayne took the silencer pistol from Quinn.

Ten minutes passed before a heavy shuffling of feet on the gravel could be discerned. Quinn leaned out carefully for a look. He pulled back, whispering, "It's Fat Pauly!"

Terry nodded to Dwayne. "Do what you gotta do. If me and Quinn have to do this job, you're gonna be as bad off as that fat Wop."

Dwayne had already chambered a round into the pistol and stood waiting. He was surprised he wasn't trembling. But he did swallow hard a couple of times and had to take some deep breaths. As soon as Fat Pauly was abreast of them, both Quinn and McCarty grabbed him, and pulled the Mafioso between the trucks.

"Hey!" the gangster yelled.

Dwayne stepped up and aimed the pistol at his victim.

"Oh, shit!" Fat Pauly said.

Dwayne pulled the trigger with the muzzle inches from the gangster's face. Then he fired twice more.

At that point, Quinn and McCarthy dropped the obese victim. McCarthy stooped down and removed everything from the dead man's pockets, including the pistol in his shoulder holster. Then he got to his feet and gave the corpse a final look.

"Let's get the hell out of here!" he ordered.

Now Dwayne was almost panting as the memory of killing Fat Pauly eased out of his mind. There were murders later on, other killings happening in a lodge during *Operation Undercover.*

On one memorable night pops could be heard out in the halls. Dwayne looked out the bedroom door to see two men firing silenced pistols into the rooms where the two gate guards were sleeping. Dwayne reached for his submachine gun and squeezed out two quick bursts that spun Pegna and Bonvicini completely around before they crumpled under the fusillade.

Downstairs in the kitchen Pablo Lazzoni, amid the five Forzinis, heard the loud shots. "What the fuck?"

Jimmy Sheehan appeared in the door. Having no military training with the submachine gun, he pulled the trigger and held it down causing the barrel to whirl wildly as it spit bullets. Spina, Viola, and Leonardi went down, but Pablo and Peachy managed to shoot back. Sheehan crumpled to the floor.

Suddenly it was quiet.

The ferociousness of the two gangsters evaporated. They looked at each other. "D'you think there's any more of 'em?" Peachy asked.

Pablo shrugged with a worried expression on his face.

Dwayne slowly eased down the stairs, holding the submachine gun ready. McCarthy followed behind to cover him. They heard some muffled talking and stopped for a quick moment, then continued. Dwayne reached the bottom of the stairs and saw Jimmy Sheehan's body in the doorway to the kitchen.

Dwayne decided to take a chance. He took a step forward, turned and squeezed the trigger four short pulls. The spread of bullets caught both Pablo and Peachy who were knocked backward to sprawl on the floor.

McCarthy joined him. "We'd better check to see if there's any more of those sons of bitches around here."

It was then that they sighted old Charlie's body in the doorway leading outside. They stepped carefully up to the opening and saw Galo draped over the banister of the stoop and Cullen and Tim Fagin sprawled on the steps. Several heavy rivulets of blood dripped to the ground below.

Dwayne and McCarthy made a slow and careful

search around the building, noting there was nobody else in the area.

"Let's check the truck," McCarthy said.

They walked from the stoop to the vehicle and looked inside. Dwayne saw the boxes. "There's a shipment of narcotics here."

"That's good," McCarthy said. He took a deep breath. "I don't know what brought on that gunfight."

"Y'know something, Terry?" Dwayne remarked. "If I learned anything from this undercover work, it's that the assholes in organized crime are their own worst enemies."

Now the recollection caused him to smile. He looked over at Donna Sue under the covers. He yawned, closed his eyes, then drifted off to sleep.

CHAPTER 9

Two Mafia Boston crime organizations—the Forzini Mob and the Lundari Gang—had lost the best of their members in what was called *Operation Undercover*. That was also the fate of the Banocci Crime Family of New York City and the Irish Derby Gang of Boston.

The fighting on the Kansas prairie was between those four East Coast criminal organizations. That made it easier for the lawmen of Kansas to score victories after victories in arresting and killing the murderers.

Now young Johnny Forzini was embarrassed by what happened to his now useless family. He had been a teenager when all that happened and he decided he wanted to get revenge on an enemy that was far from Boston. The Godfathers of the two Boston families—Angelo Lundari and Joe Forzini—had both been killed.

Johnny's best pal was Tom Lundari who was also upset by his father's fate. He and Johnny worked together for a demolition company. They were on the shovel and sledgehammer crew.

They had nothing but hatred for the local young

thugs who had no respect for the memories of the Godfathers. The punks now committed crimes like stealing hubcaps, picking pockets, rolling drunks, etc. They also tried to have sex with each other's sisters.

Johnny and Tom lived next door to each other since the Forzinis house burned down. Johnny had spent months developing a plan in order to form a new crime family. He decided to share it with Tom. Early one afternoon Johnny visited him with an idea. Tom was sitting on his stoop smoking a cigarette and drinking a Coke when his pal walked up.

"I need some help, Tom. I want to get all the guys who served our dads for a meeting."

"What about?"

"Getting even with Kansas."

"Johnny, you interest me," Tom said. "But ain't they all dead?"

"I'm talking about getting the guys who were their sons, brothers, cousins and all that."

"Well, there's not a hell of a lot of 'em. But I don't have much respect for them dipshits anymore."

"Me, either," Johnny said. "What I want to do is gather 'em up for an organizational meeting. We can pick out the good guys."

"It can be good in the back room of the Ristorante Italiana," Tom said.

"Well, the Forzini clubroom in the Ristorante Italiana is in fine shape," Johnny told him. "Let's go over there. I got a big surprise."

"Lead the way, pal."

The pair rode in Johnny's 1929 Chevy Coupe from their neighborhood into the local shopping area. Johnny knocked on the door when they reached the Ristorante Italiana. The restaurant wasn't open yet but a curtain was pulled back by somebody inside. It was elderly Carlo Tedeschi, the owner. He opened the door and let Johnny and Tom in.

He greeted them. "Hello, boys. What's cooking?"

"We hope it's for us," Johnny said with a chuckle. "How'd you like to serve some young guys who want to make their bones?"

"I am honored."

"I'll give you the date later," he said.

The old man proudly announced, "I have kept it in good shape. I knew it would be used again."

"That exactly what's happening," Johnny said. "And it's gonna be better than ever."

———

A WEEK LATER JOHNNY WAS SURPRISED BY THE appearance of his Uncle Fabio. He was a bachelor who lived in Chicago. He announced he had retired and was going on his way to live in Miami Beach, Florida.

Johnny was glad to see him because he always brought presents. This visit got his mother an expensive watch.

"I got something for you, Johnny," Uncle Fabio told him "It's all about the work I'm leaving."

"What's that?"

"I was selling yellow cigarettes."

Johnny was confused. "What are yellow cigarettes, Uncle Fabio?"

"Those are cigarettes that ain't taxed, I've got a map to show you." He got a rolled up paper. "See?"

"Yeah," Johnny said.

"This was my work. I thought you might want to see what I was doing all that time."

Johnny looked carefully at the chart. "That map shows a lot of places, Uncle Fabio."

"Yep. It starts with Panama City in Florida then goes to New Orleans, Dallas, Wichita, Kansas City and Chicago where I worked."

"Tell me about Wichita, Uncle Fabio."

"Well, I'm afraid that city was where your dad and his pals were killed."

"Can I have this map, Uncle Fabio?"

Fabio grinned. "Are you gonna get even, Johnny?"

"Maybe so, Uncle Fabio."

———

Dwayne Wheeler and Jerry Owens continued with their travels from Wichita to Kansas City delivering yellow cigarettes. Things went smoothly although Dwayne would get spasms of regret because of what was going to happen when Treasury Agents-1 and -2 lowered the boom.

Donna Sue sensed something was bothering Dwaine, but she didn't discuss it with him. Their relationship with Jerry and Melanie was like all childless couples. They did more things together such as dancing at the Roadhouse, visiting the Wichita Zoo and other amusements. Dwayne secretly dreaded that he knew all that fun would soon end.

CHAPTER 10

Johnny Forzini had been working angrily to get the Forzini and Lundari punk gangsters together. After numerous attempts, he finally managed to recruit eight volunteers. Charlie Diego, Eddie Edoardo, Roy Matteo and Manny Domenico came from the Forzini Family. The Lundaris were Ray Gabriele, Rick Riccardo, Gus Augusto and Guy Maglioni.

Johnny rented the smaller dining room of the Ristorante Italiana out of his savings. Old Carlo Tedeschi, the restaurant owner, canceled the rent on the room and only charged for the supper. Having mobsters brought back happy memories for him. The food was served at eight p.m. and the meal lasted until nine-fifteen. When the table was cleared, Johnny called for silence.

"All right, you guys," he began. "I'm gonna let you know why I brought us altogether. So! The first thing I want to say is there ain't gonna be any of this old fashion shit. You forget that! There's gonna be one name and one name only for us. *Vendetta!* Vengeance!"

The young men, happy with Italian wine, applauded.

Johnny continued, "You all know what happened to our families, right? So I'm gonna be the Boss, and Tom Lundari is gonna be the Underboss, see! The rest of you are gonna be the Soldiers, see! If you want to be a Capo someday, then you better not fuck up!"

Johnny turned to Tom. "Your turn, Underboss."

Tom spoke up loud and clear. "Carlo Tedeschi who owns this place is going to continue allowing us to use the back room. There's already a refrigerator, tables and chairs, a pool table and a dart board. There is also a shower stall, restroom, and clothing hooks. I've ordered some weights to work out with. I've advised the Boss that good physical conditioning is essential. You're going to go up against Kansas hicks and I can tell you, they're pretty damn tough."

"Thanks, Underboss," Johnny said. He turned to the others. "I want to see all you guys in the back room tomorrow."

———

DONNA SUE WAS INTERRUPTED READING THE *Women's Monthly Magazine* by the telephone. "Hello."

A man's booming voice was heard. "Hello, Donna Sue! It's me! Your old pal Peter Van Dyke!"

"Are you in Wichita?"

"I sure am and Sybil is with me in good ol' suite 206 in the Riverview Hotel."

"I remember that as your favorite one."

"It sure is. Can I speak to Dwayne, please?"

"Dwayne is out of town until tomorrow morning."

"Is he on some juicy caper?"

"He's driving a truck," Donna Sue said. "He can tell you all about it tomorrow morning."

"Okay. I'll let you speak to Sybil."

His wife Sybil was in a good mood. "Hello, Donna Sue. It seems we always come without letting you know we'll be visiting."

"As long as you get here is all that matters."

The two women fell into a feminine phone conversation that lasted forty-five minutes.

———

JOHNNY FORZINI CAME HOME FROM A GRUELING day of demolition. He went to the kitchen where his mother was drinking a cup of coffee.

He put his lunchbox down and looked at her. "Is there anything wrong?"

She stood up and picked up a flashlight off the counter. "Come with me."

They walked outside through the kitchen and Johnny pulled open the cellar door. They went down the steps and his mother pointed to the darkest corner, handing him the flashlight. "Your papa wanted me to give you some things, Johnny. I should have done it a long time ago."

He turned the flashlight on and walked over to some boxes. There was a large stiff cardboard box and he pulled off the top. He found some wrapped dollar bills inside. He was astounded. "These are all twenties!"

"Yeah, Johnny. Your papa said there was twenty-thousand dollars."

He turned to a crate. A crowbar was laying on the top. He took the tool and pried the wooden cover off. There were three Tommy guns, automatic pistols, and ammunition lying in the container. There were also ammo drums for the Tommy guns.

His mother spoke up. "It's all there, Johnny."

"Thank you, mama!"

"Johnny, *mio caro*, don't take them. *Piacere!* You will be killed like your papa!"

Johnny embraced and kissed his mother. "Don't worry. I know what I'm gonna do."

She silently left him and went upstairs to weep.

Johnny pulled the weapons and ammunition, almost dizzy with delight. He left one of the Tommy submachine guns and an ammunition drum out but packed everything else. He liked all of those more than he did the money.

CHAPTER 11

Dwayne and Donna Sue walked across the lobby of the Riverview Hotel toward the elevator. The shamus knew how to operate the conveyance and he closed the door then pushed the button for the second floor. When the couple reached the destination, they stepped out into the hallway and walked down to suite 206.

Dwayne's knocks on the door brought Sybil to open it. She showed a very happy smile. "Come on in, you two!"

This was followed by Dwayne and Pete hugging the girls and the females kissing the males. Pete said, "Guess who I've got some Jack Daniels Sour Mash Whiskey for."

"Mmm," Dwayne said with a wink. "The Pope?"

"That was close but it's you," Pete said with a chuckle at the poor joke. "I'll pour some for you, Dwayne, but first I have to mix two gin-and-tonics for a couple of beautiful women I know." He did the cocktails then poured Dwayne's whiskey and took a glass of scotch he had already drunk from. "Now let's sit down."

The men took two easy chairs while Donna Sue and Sybil settled on a settee. Pete spoke up, saying, "I've been in touch with Nigel Hawthorne. He said he'd talked with you."

"Yeah," Dwayne said. "I was with the bondsman A.J. Kessler when one of his captives tried to shoot us. We were faster. Anyhow, to make things simple, I took an Argentine money engraving and it was really Nigel's. So I gave it to him."

"He told me all about it," Pete said. He looked over at the women. "I know you gals can keep secrets, so get ready to do just that." He turned back to Dwayne. "Let me give you a real surprise."

"Are you still his boss now?"

"I've been his boss for a long time. So listen up. Nigel and I have been getting into a real legal program. And I mean *legal*!"

"Okay."

"Here's the pitch. Nigel and I are now working on a top secret project for the U.S. Government. And we have a bad guy to deal with."

"That does sound interesting."

"The bad guy is a Kraut *Waffen-SS* officer veteran by the name of Heinrich Stark," Pete said. "He is the leader of a German plot to take over several South American countries. They are Argentina, Chile, Paraguay, Bolivia and Uruguay."

"How the hell are they gonna do that?" Dwayne wanted to know.

"It involves breaking up those nation's communication and commerce. Nazi criminal organizations have taken over several South American nations' cash. They are making phony money engravings and distributing them to Latin-American governments. I mentioned the money they have now is not reliable because of those illegal forgers. Those Krauts don't have the best operations. So we are running them out with our more sophisticated commodity."

"I've been there," Dwayne said.

"It sounds like hell itself, so I've decided to stay here in Wichita at the Riverside Hotel," he explained. "I've rented an office on the top floor to run things. It's a luxurious one room with a thick carpet and modish and trendy furniture."

Sybil added, "We've got a wonderful view of the Big Arkansas River."

"It's really nice, no kidding," Pete said. "I've set up a shortwave radio on a table in the office. The call sign is AAX-Twenty-Three. When I want to get in touch with Nigel his call sign is AAZ-Zero-Three."

"That sounds like a government or commercial setup," Dwayne said.

"Let me tell you something, Dwayne. We're working for the United States Government like I said." Pete finished off his scotch. "I'm hoping I can get you to take part in this project. We have a building that was used for codebreakers during the war. It's a fortress that Nigel and Rhone found and set up." He paused. "I won't talk about that anymore."

Dwayne and Donna Sue exchanged looks, then the shamus said, "I can't work for you. I'm under the heavy fist of the United States Treasury."

"Christ! What the hell have you gotten into?"

"I'll make it quick. I sold some yellow cigarettes to some guys I wanted to get arrested for another crime. Those sales put me right under the nose of the United States Treasury. They promised not to convict me if I would go undercover in a syndicate that deals in those untaxed cigarettes. And they promised not to take away my detective license."

"Is there any way you can rush that situation?"

"Nope. And to make things worse, there's only a couple of weeks between the deliveries."

"Okay, Dwayne. We'll have to work out something or other, but I want you! Don't worry, I can contact the right people."

———

JOHNNY FORZINI DIDN'T RUSH OVER TO TOM Lundari's house to tell him what his dad had left him. He sat up late at night to do some planning for using all those guns, ammo and twenty dollar bills. After going that far, Johnny took the stuff out of the cellar and carried it up to his bedroom.

He spent a week getting his strategy wrapped up. Then it happened on a Friday afternoon when he and Tom were riding in Johnny's old Chevy coupé to their homes after a day's work.

"Say, Tom, I'd like you to come over to my house. There's something I want to show you."

"What about?"

"You'll see."

Johnny pulled up in front of his house and he and Tom got out of the Coupé.

Tom was curious. "C'mon! What's this all about?"

"You'll see."

When they entered the house, Johnny called out, "It's me and Tom, Ma."

They went up to his bedroom and Johnny said, "You're not gonna believe your eyes when you see it."

"Is it a porn collection?"

"Don't be so goddamn silly!" Johnny scolded him. He walked over to his closet and kneeled down. He stood up and carried a large cardboard box over to his bed. He opened it up and said, "How's this for your eyes?"

Tom's jaw dropped. "Holy shit! Is that real money?"

"You bet your butt it's real! Twenty thousand dollars all in twenty dollar bills. A thousand of 'em. And they ain't counterfeit."

"Where'd you get this?"

"It's from my dad. And now get ready for another surprise!"

He got on his knees and reached into the closet. He took a deep breath, then pulled out a crate that had a crowbar on top. "You're gonna really like this!" He took the tool and pried the lid off. The three Tommy guns with ammo drums and ten semi-automatic Beretta pistols were in the container.

Tom stepped back and sat down on the bed. "Where did you...I mean what..."

"My dad left it for me," Johnny interrupted. "My ma was afraid of it, but she finally gave it all to me." Johnny put both containers in the closet and sat down with Tom. "We're gonna have to get serious now. Okay? I'm the Boss, and you're the Underboss."

"That *really* means something now, Johnny."

"Yeah! And we can quit knocking down buildings for a living."

"Mmm," Tom was thinking. "We need the first Capo. D'you have any ideas?"

"Sure. Gus Augusto. He's a big muscular guy who's tough as nails. Gus is a champion bodybuilder. And he also does competition weightlifting. He scores high in that, too."

"He ain't real bright, Johnny."

"That's what makes him perfect. He'll do everything we tell him to do."

"How're we gonna get this rolling?"

"We'll start with another meeting in the Ristorante Italiana," Johnny said. "You and me will have to keep an eye on every one of them guys. If either you or me don't like the looks of somebody, then off he goes. If we liked another candidate, he'll stay and be a Soldier."

"I'm sure looking forward to shooting them Tommy guns."

"We got to shoot them pistols first," Johnny said. "We can take the Soldiers down to Guido's Gun Store. He's got a pistol range in the basement." He paused and frowned. "Just keep in mind like I told you. We're gonna have to get rid of the guys that don't measure up to being Soldiers."

"Yeah. We're gonna have to rub out some local guys, huh?"

"No we can't," Johnny said. "I don't want to piss off any neighborhood people. So we'll scare those guys into keeping their mouths shut."

CHAPTER 12

Pete Van Dyke was in his hotel office warming up his shortwave radio. He took the microphone and spoke into it. "AAC-Zero-Three. AAC-Zero-Three. This is AAX-Twenty-Three."

Nigel Hawthorne replied. "AAC-Zero-Three. I hear you loud and clear."

"There's a problem with Dwayne. He's gotten into trouble with the Federal Treasury Department."

Nigel asked, "How much?"

"Really bad. That's why I'm letting you know we've got a big problem here. I'll try to work things out since I'm staying at the Riverside Hotel in Wichita"

"I'm pretty busy what with the engravers and guards. I'll also have five courtesans coming in on the next aeroplane to keep those men happy. The two cooks are man and wife along with two young Mexican boys who are getting their food supply shipped into the Waldo grocery store. And they are getting it from Ness City up north."

"Sounds good. AAX-Twenty-Three. Out."

Pete laid the microphone down and looked at Sybil

sitting in front of his desk. "Damn! This operation must have Dwayne in it. He's too talented to go to waste."

"Why don't you grab hold of him and send him over to Nigel?"

"We would have too much to lose," Pete said. "The best thing I can do at this moment is to contact him here in Wichita now and then."

"That's a good idea, Pete. I'll bet he's probably trying to get out of his problem and link up with you."

"If it can be done," Pete said, "Dwayne Wheeler can do it."

————

JOHNNY MADE ARRANGEMENTS TO SET UP another supper in the Ristorante Italiana's private dining room. Carlo Tedeschi, thrilled at entertaining the Mafia again, laid out a sumptuous menu. *Antipasto, Calamari Fritta,* (deep fried calamari), *Specialita Della Casa: Melanzane Rollantinge* (eggplant stuffed and rolled with ricotta), and lastly *Cannoli* for dessert.

The dinner was scheduled for 8 p.m.

The eight young men invited were looking forward to another delicious supper. The *cucina* of the Ristorante Italiana was noted for its delicious food. It was said that if old Carlo Tedeschi could raise the money he could set up a restaurant that would be the best in Boston.

Johnny Forzini had put place cards on the plates. He and Tom Lundari had arranged it so the that there were three tables. The number one table seated Boss Johnny Forzini, Underboss Tom Lundari, and the newly appointed Capo Gus Augusto. When he received the raise in rank the day before, he had wept with pride.

The second table was for the more trusted four to be

Soldiers. They were Charlie Giego, Eddie Edoardo, Rick Riccardo and Guy Maglioni. Sitting at the third table was Roy Matteo, Manny Domenico and Roy Gabriele who were not considered trustworthy or very smart.

The food was served at a quarter past 8 p.m. The diners talked and laughed loud except for the Boss, the Underboss and the Capo. They kept an eye on the others to judge their personalities. One important way to judge a man is how he acts when he gets drunk. A guy who is calm and quiet, generally can be trusted even when guzzling alcoholic liquor. But if he's drunk and loud, it shows he has no self-control.

By the time the dessert was served, Roy Matteo, Manny Domenico and Ray Gabriela were talking loud and acting boisterously. All of them were seated at that same table. The other table Charlie Diego, Eddie Edoardo, Rick Riccardo, and Guy Maglioni, had been telling some jokes and laughing.

More wine was served while the tables were being cleared. At that point, Johnny Forzini stood up and tapped his glass with a spoon. "*Attenzione! Attenzione!* Let's get organized, okay? I have a most important announcement to make." He nodded to Gus Augusto to get to his feet. Johnny continued, "Gus Augusto has been appointed Capo of the Vendetta Family."

Matteo, Domenico and Gabriela were called over to the table where Johnny, Tom and Gus were seated.

Gus, as Capo, frowned at them. "You three guys ain't worth shit. As the Capo I'm warning you to watch your manners. One mistake and you guys are gonna get a hit and I mean by bullets, see?"

The trio's faces paled. The fear they felt sobered them up.

"Get out of here and don't come back!"

The three made a quick exit.

———

JOHNNY, TOM, AND GUS WERE IN THE BACK room early the next morning. They gathered around the card table and waited for the coffee to percolate. Tom had bought a box of donuts, but just him and Johnny ate them. Gus was a health nut and he ate muscle-building cookies. Johnny and Tom drank coffee.

"Okay," Johnny said. "Let's get this over with. He reached in a box he had brought with him. He pulled out three Beretta pistols and shoved one to each member of the staff across the table. "I got bullets in my coat. You can put 'em in the magazines when you get the chance." He passed out sixty bullets each. "Don't worry. There's a hell of a lot more of 'em."

"What about holsters?" Tom asked.

"We're going to do target shooting in Guido Calo's basement range from here now," Johnny said. "So we can buy some in his store. I made arrangements for that. Guido was happy to help out. He said he wouldn't take any money."

"Hey, Johnny," Gus said. "What about Charlie, Eddie, Rick, and Guy?"

"I want to keep the Officers ahead of the Soldiers. They can do some shooting a little later. They'll be okay when we make war on Wichita."

"You're right," Johnny remarked. "But first us three guys have got to do some learning on our part." He looked at his watch. "Gather the pistols and bullets. Guido will want us to get there early."

———

JOHNNY, TOM, AND GUS WALKED INTO GUIDO Calo's Gun Shop. His son was dealing with a customer. He interrupted his sales talk to turn his head toward the office. "Hey, Pop, Johnny and his buddies are here."

Guido came out happily grinning. "Johnny and Tom, how are you? Who's your pal?"

"This is Gus Augusto," Johnny answered.

"Glad to know you, Gus. Well, c'mon, let's go down to the basement and make some noise."

"We'd like to buy some shoulder holsters first, Guido."

"What have you got to stick in 'em, guys?"

The three reached in their jacket pockets and pulled out the Berettas and laid them on the counter. "This is what we got," Johnny said.

"Where did you buy those pistols?" Guido asked. "They're damn fine weapons."

Johnny spoke up. "My dad left 'em for me."

"Mmm!" Guido said in admiration. "These compact pistols are the Beretta 1934s. They're easy for concealment under a suit coat." He went back to the end of the counter and returned with the leather objects. "Try 'em on, guys."

The trio took off their jackets and slipped into the holsters. After buckling the straps, they slipped their pistols into the leather pockets.

Johnny grabbed his Beretta and pulled the weapon out. Then the three of them did the movement several times.

"How d'you like 'em," Guido asked.

"These will do just fine," Johnny said. Tom and Gus agreed.

"Okay," Guido said. "Now let's go downstairs to the basement. That's where the targets are."

The shooting range was ten yards long and there were

a dozen stations with tables. The shooters pulled out their sixty-bullet boxes and opened them up before setting them down on the ledges at the shooting stations.

Guido showed them how to load the magazines. The capacities were seven rounds.

"Now," Guido said. "Take the shooting stance like this." He showed them how. "Aim toward the targets using the sights. Okay? What eyes are yours."

"What's that?" Johnny asked.

"Okay. Aim at the targets with both eyes and look at the target. Now aim with you left eye, then your right eye. Which one is accurate?"

"My left eye was on the target," Johnny said.

"Mine, too," Tom reported.

"Then those are the eyes you will aim with."

Gus was worried. "My right eye was on the target."

"That's fine," Guido said. "That's the eye you will want to shoot with." He cleared his throat. "Ready! Aim! Fire!"

The three squeezed their triggers and the target shooting started.

CHAPTER 13

The sound of the C-47 could be heard in the distance. Then the noise grew louder. The pilot Larry Bradford raised the shortwave radio in his cockpit to talk with Nigel Hawthorne. His mechanic Harold Anderson settled in for the landing.

Bradford lowered the wheels. "Them guys are gonna get a real nice surprise."

Down on the runway Nigel replied, "AAC-Zero-Three. Everything is okay for a landing."

Bradford said, "Roger. Coming in. Building is in sight."

The airplane was landed perfectly and taxied up to the door of the building. The pilot and Harold Anderson stepped out and turned to help five young and attractive Mexican women to disembark. The pilot pulled their five suitcases out and set them down. They were dressed in a sexy way and showed very happy attitudes. These females were prostitutes out of a high-priced bordello in Mexico City. It was Nigel Hawthorne who hired the women.

Without them there would be no sex and that would have been a bad problem.

The five young artist engravers had been waiting for their arrival. They trotted out to the airplane, eager to greet them. Fritz Harrigan, Stanley Morris, Robbie Lewis, Frank Watson, and Jimmy Staunton picked up the women's luggage.

The engravers and women went to the third floor to where the narrow bedrooms were situated. The ladies of the night waited while their luggage was laid down on the bunks.

Nigel Hawthorne appeared. "I say, you chaps. You can see those tarts later this evening. Now get back to your engraving chores." He turned to leave, then turned back. "I should remind you that you will share the five ladies with the ten guards. I will not tolerate any shenanigans where these women are concerned. They are being presented to you for your relaxation and fun. Understand?"

The young men knew Hawthorne was a strict disciplinarian. "Yes, Mister Hawthorne," they all intoned.

———

DWAYNE WHEELER AND JERRY OWENS DROVE through the Kansas night. They had developed a close friendship because of the way their wives got along so well. During their travels they planned on what they wanted to do between trips. They had just discussed going to Wichita University Saturday football games when Jerry smirked.

"What's the problem?" Dwayne asked.

"We ain't gonna see a football game," Jerry said. "And you know it."

"Yes. I know it. All our girls want is movies, eating at restaurants, and taking canoes out on the Big Arkansas."

"Y'know, Dwayne, I'd like to go to one of the wrestling matches at the Forum."

"Are you crazy!"

"Well...maybe."

Dwayne chuckled. "There ain't no way that Donna Sue would want to go to a wrestling match."

"I suppose that's the same with Melanie."

Dwayne lit a Lucky Strike cigarette. "I see the rising sun in the east. I'll take over the driving now."

———

A LOUD RUMBLING AND FIGHTING BROKE OUT ON the third floor of the old codebreaker building. The engravers and off-duty guards were having an argument, yelling at each other with threats. Their anger was scaring the five hookers so badly that they had gotten together, trembling in one bedroom.

Nigel Hawthorne and retired Regimental Lieutenant Major Herbert Rhodes charged into the mob, slashing their swagger sticks right and left. They broke up the fighting in a quick way.

"All right, you scum," Rhodes voice boomed. "Stop where you are!"

The fighters stood panting. Some had red welts across their faces and others had torn shirts.

Rhodes used his swagger stick pointing where he wanted them to go. "Engravers there! Guards there!" With that he addressed Hawthorne. "They're yours, sir."

Hawthorne glared at the ruffled group. "Evidently you took no mind in what I told you when the ladies arrived. I know you all are horny and anxious." He pointed at the one bedroom where the terrorized tarts stood, huddled tight together. "Those ladies are scared out of their wits. It wouldn't surprise me if they wanted to be flown back to Mexico City." He paused and glared even more. "Tell me! Do you want these tarts to do that? To go back to Mexico City?" The brawlers stood silent. "Well! Goddamn your souls! If that's what you want, say so."

Fritz Harrigan raised his hand. "I'd like to have them here, sir."

Another hand was raised. Then another. Then two more. Then every hand was raised.

Hawthorne turned to Rhodes. "Do you still have that roster you made this afternoon?"

"Yes, sir!"

"Read it to these miserable bastards."

"Yes, sir." He pulled a roster from his shirt pocket and cleared his throat. "There will not be any sex Saturdays and Sundays. Now! The first rank to visit the whores will be Monday night for the following engravers. Harrigan, Morris and Watson. Tuesday will be the guards Blevins, O'Riley, Dixon, Ruff, Splatt, and Jeff Jones. Wednesday will be the night off for the other blokes. Thursday will be engravers Lewis, Staunton and Harris. The Friday ranks will be the guards Williams, Carter, Jackson, Acton and Howard."

Nigel Hawthorne folded his arms over his chest. "If there is any more trouble I will have a guillotine built to lop off bloody heads. Just to make things right, we'll start calling this place headquarters. Got it? *The Headquarters!*"

CHAPTER 14

At the end of a work week, Johnny Forzini and Tom Lundari quit their demolition jobs. They were at the shack waiting to get their final pay packets.

Superintendent Miskoski handed them their money. "I'm really pissed off about your guys quitting."

"We got good reasons, Miskoski."

"You guys are nuts," Miskoski grumbled. "If you quit you'll lose your pensions."

Tom spoke up. "We're gonna have a hell of a lot more money than pensions."

"We've chose another line of work," Johnny said.

"For Christ sake," Miskoski said. "You can't leave me now! This job ain't half done."

"Sorry," Johnny said.

They walked out of the work yard feeling like a ton of bricks had been lifted off them. "Are you ready for it?" Johnny said.

"Ready for what?" Tom said.

"Ready for me buying a car."

"You bet! That'll be a surprise for Sofia and Maria."

Johnny lit a cigarette. "Maybe they'll start putting out, huh?"

"Forget that. They're nice Catholic girls."

They walked over to the parking area of the destruction area and got into Johnny's 1929 Chevy Coupé.

"When are you going for the new car?

"I've already bought it," Johnny said. "It's waiting for me over at Pegna Used Cars. The dealer Giovanni is gonna have one of his guys clean it. It's really a 1941 Ford sedan and it's been took good care of."

"You'll buy a brand new car as soon as they make 'em now that the war is over," Tom said. "It won't be long."

Johnny drove onto the Giovanni Used Cars parking area. The two young men got out of the Coupé. "Giovanni!" Johnny used the man's first name.

The car salesman walked around Johnny's Chevy. "You've taken good care of that car. I can fix it up pretty good to sell."

"Well, I got other plans for it," Johnny said. He turned to Tom and handed him the keys of the Chevy Coupé. "This is yours, pal."

"Maria is gonna like that a lot!" Tom intoned. "I can take her for car rides now!"

————

CHARLIE AND JANET MEADOWS WERE THE husband and wife who did all the cooking in the code building. They were a middle-aged couple and were excellent cooks. They had been with Nigel Hawthorne for five years in his Chicago house and now they followed him to Kansas.

The first thing the couple did was to go to the Waldo

grocery store. They made arrangements to get food orders from the market in Ness City.

The arrival of the Mexican women had added to the meals. The couple got into the company's jeep and drove over to the small town of Waldo to pick up some grocery shopping.

As Charlie motored down the road, he noticed that Janet wasn't speaking. "What's wrong?"

"I don't like those sinful women who have joined us."

"Well, the engravers and the guards are hale and hearty," he explained. "Young men like them have got to have sex. That's it! Period!"

Janet knew that her husband was right. "Well, I'm sure they'll settle down."

They approached the town of Waldo, where there was a grocery store, diner, filling station and small scattering of a half dozen houses. Charlie turned off the road and drove up to the grocery.

Harold Drake, the grocery man and town clerk, looked up and gave the visitors a friendly greeting when they walked in. "Hello, there, folks. Your order has arrived. I put the cold stuff in my refrigerator."

"We appreciate that, Harold," Charlie said.

"One of these days, I'll find out what you government folks are doing."

"Oh, sure!" Charlie said with a laugh. "President Truman will call you up to spill the beans."

Janet walked over to the bookrack and picked out three women's magazines.

She called over to Charlie. "There's some men's reading material here. Football and hunting. You want me to get 'em?"

"Sure and a couple of comics. Superman and Batman."

Charlie carried the food order to the jeep then headed back to the code building.

———

THE CLUB DELUXE WENT BACK TO THE EARLY days of Prohibition and was so elegant and opulent that no gangster would dare start trouble in it. A dance band that had been playing since the beginning, offered many melodies that went from 1920 to the 1940s. The bar boasted the best in cocktails, champagnes and liquors. Additionally, the food served were different luxurious hors d'oeuvres.

Mr. and Mrs. Joe Forzini along with Mr. and Mrs. Angelo Lundari had been happy patrons. But *Operation Undercover* put an end to that.

———

JOHNNY FORZINI AND TOM LUNDARI WERE IN their individual homes dressing in their best and only suits. The duo had showered, shaved and shined their shoes. Tom checked his suit then went over to Johnny's house, where Johnny had been waiting for him. The two got into Johnny's Ford and headed for a florist they'd seen in the neighborhood.

The lady who owned the shop watched them as they entered her store. The pair strolled around trying to figure out what to buy. The shop manager knew they had no idea what they were doing.

She walked around the counter. "What are you boys looking for?"

"We really don't know," Johnny confessed.

"Well then, what's the occasion?"

"My buddy bought a new car a lot bigger than his old one," Tom told her. "We're going to surprise our two girlfriends and we're going to take them dancing."

"Alright," the lady said. "I tell you what. Why not buy the young ladies corsages?"

"What's corsages?" Johnny asked.

"They are small bouquets to pin to their dresses. I have some over here."

She took them to a glass display. "I suggest that you buy two different kinds. One for each young lady."

"Okay!" Johnny said, liking her idea.

They waited as she chose the right flowers and put them each in a cellophane sack. The two friends paid for the bouquets and left the shop eagerly wanting to see what the girls would think.

From there they went the short distance to Sofia Vanacore's house. Maria Palma would be there, too. Their parents insisted on that arrangement so that one couple would not be alone.

The pair went up to the door and rang the bell. Mrs. Vanacore answered the door. She gave the two boys a quick going over. The lady liked the looks of the bouquets. She called out, "Your guys are here."

The girls came to the door and were pleased to see the corsages. "Wow!" Maria said. "They're so beautiful. How come you guys never did this before?"

"The lady in her shop helped us with them."

After pinning the florals on them, the quartet walked out the door and down to the sidewalk. The girls were confused. "Where's your car?" Sofia asked Johnny.

"Surprise! There's my new car!" Johnny sang out. The guys escorted them to the car and everyone got in. He stuck the key in the ignition, turned it and pulled away from the curb.

"Where are we going?" Sofia asked.

"We got reservations," Johnny said. "At the Club Deluxe on the southern side of Cambridge."

The girls squealed in delight as Johnny drove. Tom put his arm around Sofia and began kissing her. She returned his ardor, then broke the embrace. "Hey, Tommy! Don't put your hands down there!"

"C'mon, sweetie!" Tom said. "We're going big shot tonight. The Club Deluxe has been running hot and heavy since prohibition."

"That don't mean you can do what you want with me."

Johnny looked at Maria in the car's mirror. "I got in touch with an old friend of my and Tom's dads. Otherwise we couldn't get in. That's a jazzy joint."

"Yeah," Sofia said. "C'mon, Maria! You don't want to be a party pooper."

Johnny, Tom and the girls traveled on a road that led into a forested area. Johnny slowed down as they rolled up to a fence. A couple of extremely large men were manning the gate.

One walked up. "Hey, you kids! Turn around and skedaddle."

Johnny wasn't worried. "I was supposed to tell you that we're Forzini and Lundari."

"Oh! I used to know your dads and moms a long time ago." He looked over at the other man. "Let 'em in, Tony."

Johnny drove up to the front door. He stopped and got out, leaving the motor running. Tom and the two girls exited the car on the other side. The parking attendant handed a ticket to Johnny.

The quartet walked up to the front door and were stopped at the maître d' station.

Johnny announced, "Forzini and Lundari."

The maître d' checked his list, then said. "Come with me, if you please."

The other diners were amazed to see high school girls being escorted to one of the best tables. The men noted that the young males appeared older and more mature than their dates. The pair also had an aura of toughness that gave them the look of Mafiosos.

A waiter appeared with four menus and waited patiently as the young ladies were flabbergasted at the offerings. Johnny took over and ordered four shrimp and sardines on lettuce. There was a saucy dip to add to the flavor. The waiter suggested a Chardonnay wine. Johnny thanked him and the waiter retired to fill their order.

The dance band appeared for its first performance as the musicians took their instruments. They opened the program with *The Continental.*

Johnny and Tom took their dates onto the floor to begin an evening of dancing.

The four young people enjoyed the band's first performance then went back to the four luxurious foods waiting for them at the table.

It was going to be a wonderful evening.

———

AFTER THE TIME WAS CLOSE TO ELEVEN P.M., THE two girls insisted that they be taken home. Maria Palma always stayed in Sofia Vanacore's home after their dates with the boys. This was ordered by their parents so that they would be sure to stay together.

CHAPTER 15

It was on a Sunday morning when Boss Johnny Forzini sat down in the back room of the Ristorante Italiana with his gang. Carlo Tedeschi, owner of the restaurant, had served them some coffee and *Pasticceria* pastry.

"Let me see who's here," Johnny said with a wink. "There's me the Boss, the Underboss Tom Lundari, Capo Gus Augusto, and Soldiers Charlie Giego, Eddie Edoardo, Guy Maglioni, and Rick Ricardo." He grinned and stood up, looking around. "Is that everybody?"

"What about the alley cat outside?" Tom said with a chuckle.

"He's on guard duty," Johnny said. "So we're safe. And now let's get down to business." He opened a brief-case and pulled out a rolled-up piece of paper. "This, gentlemen, is a very important map. I got this from my Uncle Fabio while he was passing through Boston. It is the operations of an outfit that is peddling cigarettes. Special cigarettes that is! They got no tax paid on 'em."

Charlie Giego was curious. "Are we gonna take that outfit over?"

"Only in one place," Johnny said. He paused and uttered, "Wichita, Kansas!"

"What about Wichita, Kansas?" Guy Maglioni asked.

"Kansas is where our dads were killed by the law a coupla years ago," Johnny said. "Not a one of them survived and that includes the Capos and Soldiers."

Charlie Giego raised his hand. "We all know about that, Boss. Are we gonna steal that cigarette outfit in Wichita?"

"No," Johnny said. "We're gonna wipe out those Wichita bastards, then let the other outfits try to figure out what happened. That would be Panama City, Florida; New Orleans, Louisiana; Dallas, Texas; Kansas City, Missouri, and last but not least Chicago, Illinois. They're all here on this map." He paused. "I'll let Tom explain further."

"Okay. I got some information from Tom's Uncle Fabio. Them cigarette peddlers make two runs a month starting from Panama City. They always go the same way through the boondocks. That keeps them from running through areas that have cops, state highways, U.S. highways or a lot of population. It makes the trips a hell of a lot longer, but also a hell of a lot safer."

"How are they hauling them smokes?" Charlie asked.

"They've got special trucks," Tom said. "Johnny's Uncle Fabio explained each outfit had one 1936 Chevy 1.5-ton hauler." He grinned. "And listen! There's Hershey bars painted on their side. That fools folks that see it coming and going. They just think it's got candy."

Johnny stepped in. "Now me, Tom and Gus know you guys have jobs and can't run off to someplace right away. Eddie and Guy work at the Sereno Bakery; Rick has a job at Giovonni's Filling Station and Charlie is a janitor at the Conforto Building. You're gonna have to keep them jobs for a while, so I'm gonna give each of you Soldiers fifty bucks. How's that?"

The four showed their appreciation with whistles and applause.

Johnny continued, "Me and Tom have already quit our jobs and Gus is self-employed. So we're gonna do some traveling, observation and planning. Once we reach Kansas City we'll use Uncle Fabio's map and find a spot where them Wichita bastards will be close enough to turn the Tommy guns on them. Then we'll head back to Boston and get the Soldiers to lay the ambush with us. After the attack we'll go to Wichita and shoot up their warehouse."

———

DONNA SUE WAS RELAXING ON AN EARLY afternoon in their apartment when the telephone rang. She answered the call and recognized who was on the other line. She looked over at Dwayne. "It's your Treasury Agent-1."

Dwayne took the handset. "What's up?"

"We need a meeting," the Treasury guy said. "Meet us in Linwood Park on Bayley Street."

"Now?"

"Hell yes, *now!*"

"I'm on my way," Dwayne said. He looked at Donna Sue. "I got to go and meet them guys in Linwood Park."

"Have fun."

"I'm sure it'll be a real lot of fun."

He grabbed his hat and keys and left the apartment to walk over to the EZ Park Garage. Twenty minutes later he turned off Harry and onto Bayley Street. He spotted the agents' car and pulled up behind them, getting out at the curb.

Treasury Agent-1 said, "Let's take a walk. We don't want people to wonder what three men in a car are doing. There's been some changes in our operation. Everything has ground to a stop."

Treasury Agent-2 said, "We found out who makes those cigarettes. It's in Cuba. That's why they're making an excellent product."

"I never smoked one," Dwayne said.

"I have," Treasury Agent-1 said, "just to taste. They're actually a smooth smoke. Anyhow, they've had several shipments hijacked in Panama City and New Orleans. And another distributor has taken over. Thus, the cigarettes in Panama City are running low. In fact, too low to keep operating."

"Who's doing the looting?" Dwayne asked.

"We don't know and we got to find out and get them back to normal."

"Okay," Dwayne said. "I got a question that's not exactly about this. My driving partner Jerry Owens is a great guy. He's reliable and he served in World War Two as an infantry soldier. I feel lousy about him going to the penitentiary when this is all over. His wife Melanie and my Donna Sue have gotten to be good gal pals."

"Hell no!" Treasury Agent-1 snapped. "This Owens is a criminal."

"Alright then, Goddamn it!" Dwayne snarled. "Then I want to get a temporary job that was offered to me."

"So what?" Treasury Agent-1 asked.

"So I'm gonna take it. This is a legit outfit. Just to prove it, he has a shortwave radio. His call sign is AAX-23." He stopped. "Well, damn your eyes, you better write that down so you can get a hold of me."

Treasury Agent-1 spoke to his partner. "Write it down."

Dwayne said, "AAX-23." He checked his watch then walked back to his station wagon.

"Do you think telling him to go would be the best thing to do," Treasury Agent-2 asked.

"We can't. If we arrested him, any lawyer could get him off in the same day."

Treasury Agent-2 sighed. "Yeah. I guess you're right."

————

JOHNNY FORZINI, TOM LUNDARI AND GUS Augusto piled into Johnny's Ford on a rainy morning. They had plenty of money and a roadmap that would keep them on the better highways. Tom had gotten a map and used his ruler to measure it. They would have to drive 1500 miles from Boston to Kansas City. Johnny's uncle's map would be used by itself to see the routes of the cigarette runners.

The first day they took U.S. 20 up to Syracuse and ate lunch at a café in Albany. Capo Gus wouldn't eat the fare. His food was the healthy type and he had boxes and jars of nutritious diets.

"Do you really like that stuff, Gus?" Tom asked.

"Some of it tastes bad, but most is delicious, I don't eat it all the time."

They got back on the highway and spotted a motor court to stop at Columbus, Ohio. They got a room with two beds and a roller bed. There was a restaurant down the street where they ate. The travelers went back to the motor court and all took showers. After being refreshed, they fell into a deep sleep. All except for Capo Gus who had brought some dumbbell weights with him. He did an hour of exercise then laid on the roller bed and slept soundly.

The next morning, they woke up hungry and checked out of the motor lodge. Then, after eating big breakfasts at the same restaurant where they ate the evening before, they were refreshed and eager to get back on the highways.

It was Johnny's turn to drive on U.S. Highway 40 until he reached Indianapolis. They stayed on the outskirts of the city and ate at a diner. After eating, Tom stayed on the same highway until they reached Saint Louis where they ate again, then found another motor court.

"Okay, guys," Johnny said, spreading Uncle Fabio's map. "Tomorrow we're gonna arrive in Kansas City." He put his finger on the spot. "That's where we're gonna find the place to blast them Wichita bastards in their fucking truck! Then we'll go into that city and take out their building. That's on the map, too."

According to Uncle Fabio's map, the cigarette trucks would arrive during darkness. Johnny drove into that area to find a good place to set up an ambush and fight a battle with their Tommy guns.

Chapter 16

D onna Sue Wheeler née Connors and Sybil Van Dyke née Baldwin were off on a ladies' fine shopping excursion while their husbands were working on the highest floor of the Riverview Hotel.

Before the ladies were finished gently attacking their shops, they had visited Peacock Shoes, Helzberg Diamond Shop, Rorabaugh's Department Store, Henry's, Wards, S.G Homes and Sons, Ray Gumm Jewelry, Gateway Sporting Goods, Jenkins Music, and The Gore Hat Works. They stopped shopping once to get a quick lunch at Dockum Drugs located on the southeast corner of Douglas and Broadway.

While all that was going on, Pete Van Dyke was sitting at his desk drinking coffee with Dwayne Wheeler sitting on a nearby sofa. Pete was giving him the lowdown on the entire job he was about to get into.

"Okay, Dwayne, here's the pitch. As I told you, you'll be working for the United States Government. The reason behind this is because there are certain nations in South America who have had their economy knocked to hell through counterfeit money. That's number one. Number two is counterfeit money from a hidden Nazi Germany being spent. That's being done by local criminals. Those two organizations are tearing up a whole part of South America. We are fighting back with our skilled engravers. Those young guys are talented and fast."

"How many countries are catching hell? You told me once."

"Let's see," Pete said. He reached in his desk drawer and took out a thick pad of paper. "Here we go. Bolivia, Chile, Argentina, Paraguay, and Uruguay, all in the lower part of South America. The local counterfeit crooks are laughable, but the Nazis use excellent paper and almost perfect engraving plates."

"Wait a minute," Dwayne said. "I thought Nazi Germany was defeated."

"Not really," Pete said. "There's a small *Waffen-SS* unit trying to take over somewhere in Argentina."

"What can we do about that? "Dwayne asked.

"I've told you about the allied wartime code building that was closed up. We now refer to it by the words *The Headquarters.* Our mutual friend Nigel and his crew took it over and put it in full operation."

"I thought that when I returned the two engraving plates to him."

"By the way, there's a Wichitan who is the chief of the engravers. His name is Fritz Harrigan. You know him, right?"

"Hell, yes!" Dwayne said. "We went to East High School together. He was making engraving plates of Nazi certificates down in that basement of a house in Wichita. He was a prisoner."

"That's the one, alright."

"When he was rescued, he went to New York and became a damned fine artist," Dwayne said.

"Well, he didn't last long as an *artiste*," Pete informed him. "He was damned good at engraving, but that was only when he was doing money and legal tender. One time when Sybil and I were walking around looking at art in Greenwich Village we saw him sitting on the sidewalk selling his art. Sybil didn't know him but I did from his work on that Kraut currency."

"I remember him as a skinny, bashful kid."

"Well, you're in for a surprise when you see him," Pete said. "He got tired of being pushed around and he went to a karate studio to take training or whatever they call it. I don't know much about that martial art, but he is dangerous now. That's only if he's picked on, however." He took a cigarette out of his pack and offered it to Dwayne.

"I only smoke Lucky Strike."

"I should have remembered that," Pete said, lighting a Pall Mall. "Okay. We'll complete your education tomorrow when we fly to *The Headquarters*. We can take the girls with us."

"Who's gonna fly us?"

"I am, Dwayne. I got a pilot's license two years ago. I can rent a Cessna at the Wichita Municipal Airport."

"Wow! I'm pleasantly surprised."

Pete turned on his shortwave radio and let it warm up. As soon as the communication instrument was ready, Pete spoke into the microphone. "AAX-23 to AAC-03. I say again. AAX-23 to AAC-03."

"This is AAC-03."

"This is AAX-23. I'll be flying to *The Headquarters* early morning tomorrow. I should be landing in the afternoon."

"This is AAC-03. We'll be looking for you, AAX-23."

"This is AAX-23. Out."

———

JOHNNY FORZINI WAS LOOKING OUTSIDE THE CAR as Tom Lundari drove slowly along the rural road. "Man!" he said. "I'll bet this track is nothing but mud when it rains."

"Yeah," Gus said from the back seat.

"Wait a minute!" Johnny said suddenly.

Tom came to a quick stop. "What's up?"

Johnny got out of the car and looked around. "Hey, you guys! Take a look! There's a hump going over this ditch."

"I see," Tom said, getting next to Gus. "It probably fills up with water when it rains."

"I checked this map and the Wichita to Kansas City shipment will be passing through this very spot during night hours," Johnny said. "Look around. It's a rugged route so they'll be going slow and careful."

"You're right," Gus said. "It'll be easy to use the Tommy guns on it."

"The schedule on the map says it'll be two weeks before it gets here," Johnny said. "We got plenty of time to go back to Boston and get the Soldiers."

"I bet they're ready to go to war," Gus said.

"Yeah," Tom agreed. "After we wipe out the truck and the guys in it, we can head for Wichita and kill the rest of those bastards in their warehouse."

"Yeah!" Johnny said. "*Vendetta!* Vengeance!" He rolled up the map. "C'mon, you guys. We don't have to follow a slow route going home! We can be back there in three days!"

Chapter 17

P eter Van Dyke rented a Cessna C-37 Airmaster for the trip to *The Headquarters*. There was room for light luggage behind the passenger seats in the cabin. Donna Sue and Sybil settled down in the back while Pete and Dwayne sat in the front.

Pete started the engine and put on earphones. He contacted the tower and was given the O.K. to take off. He moved out to the runway then braked with both pedals and pulled the throttle out to full. Ten seconds later, he released the brakes and was gaining speed. He eased back on the yoke and the airplane went airborne.

Pete leveled out at four thousand feet and reached for the navigation beam. "AAX-23 to AAC-03. I say again. AAX-23 to AAC-03."

"This is AAC-03."

"This is AAX-23. I'm on the way to *The Headquarters* so set the navigation beam. I should arrive in the early afternoon. It depends on the wind up here."

"This is AAC-03. We'll be looking for you, AAX-23."

"This is AAX-23. Out."

He sat back and Dwayne looked over at him. "How come you ain't flying this airplane?" he shouted over the roar of the engine.

"I'm on autopilot," Pete yelled back.

"I see," Dwayne said loudly. "But don't take a nap. Okay?"

Pete grinned and nodded his head affirmatively.

Dwayne looked down at the Kansas plains and was much impressed by their flatness as always. After a while he became sleepy and nodded now and then. Once he glanced back where the women were and he saw Sybil with her arm around Donna Sue, who was white as a sheet. Sybil had given her a paper bag that was one of the many furnished by the Cessna company in the airplanes it rented out. Donna Sue was upchucking into it.

The engine noise was too loud for conversation, so if Pete or Dwayne wanted to make a remark about something on the ground they nudged each other and pointed. Dwayne was beginning to enjoy the flight and he studied the instrument panel, watching it giving out information about the flight.

Pete checked his watch and went down a thousand feet. Twenty minutes later there was radio talk in the air.

"AAC-03, this is AAX-23. The beam is indicating a short distance."

"AAX-23, this is AAC-03. It reads here, too. Come on in. Out."

Pete lowered the airplane into a steady slow glide toward *The Headquarters*. He lined up with the runway by lowering the flaps. He tapped on the brake pedals as he touched down and pulled the throttle back. Nigel Hawthorne waved and walked over as the plane came to a stop.

Everyone in the aircraft felt the change in their ears.

They got out and Hawthorne shook hands with Dwayne and Pete. The women followed the men and Sybil took two paper bags and dropped them in a nearby trash barrel.

"Sorry about that," Donna Sue said.

"Ha! You should have seen me when I first went up," Sybil said. "You'll be alright now."

Hawthorne invited everyone to follow him into the mess hall. The cooks Charlie and Janet Meadows had fixed up a light lunch for the visitors. There was iced tea, ham sandwiches and a light dessert of Jell-O. When the diners had taken the chairs, the two cooks made an exit.

"We've got your rooms ready for you," Nigel said. "How long are you going to stay here?"

"A couple of days," Pete said. "We got—"

Fritz Harrigan appeared and spotted Dwayne. "Hey, partner!"

"Hey, Fritz," Dwayne replied.

The two Wichitans shook hands. Dwayne was pleased. "Wow! You ain't the little scrawny guy you used to be."

"I'm the same height," Fritz said. "Just more muscles."

"What's your job around here? An engraver?"

"What else?" Fritz said. "We got five engravers and I'm the boss. I gotta get back to work, so let's meet again before you leave."

"You got it." Dwayne went back to the table and sat down.

Pete was all business. "How are things going? Any complications?"

"Not really," Nigel said. "There was a problem with some of the guards, but we disciplined them and that settled everything."

Sybil asked, "What sort of problem, Nigel?"

"We have five prostitutes," he replied. "And they are

first class Mexican women. We've scheduled the lads when to enjoy the ladies' talents, so there's no more fighting." He looked over at Dwayne. "You should have seen young Fritz in that brawl. Did you know he was an expert in Karate?"

"Not until Pete told me earlier today," Dwayne said. "He was a scrawny kid in school. We went to Willard Elementary, Roosevelt Junior High and East High. I had to beat the crap out of smart alecks a few times who were picking on him."

At the time the visitors had finished eating, Herbert Rhodes made an entrance. "Hello. We've got your apartments ready. Your luggage is in your rooms up on the second floor. They are not exactly royalty, but you'll be comfortable."

The four followed Rhodes up the metal stairs to the bedrooms. "Here you are."

"Thanks, Rhodes," Pete said.

"Hi, Rhodes," Dwayne said. "Remember me? I was the guy that tried to steal Nigel's two engraving plates."

"Indeed I do, sir," he answered with a grin. He looked at the others. "If there's anything you need, I am at your service." He walked away to get back to his duties.

"Mmf!" Sybil said. "Prostitutes! Ugh!"

Donna Sue didn't make any remarks. This was because of Mrs. Belle Davies, a madame who had helped Dwayne and Donna Sue in the past. She called her business "Venus."

"Listen, ladies," Pete said. "There are many young men here. So they got young women who can be quite nice to them. Understand?"

"Mmf!" Sybil said again.

————

Johnny Forzini and Tom Lundari wasted no time in getting their tiny Mafioso Family together in the club house. The Capo Gus Augusta and the Soldiers, Charlie Diego, Eddie Edoardo, Rick Riccardo, and Guy Maglioni, were ready to go to war and get even with the Wichitans who killed their male relatives.

Johnny and Tom had brought the three Tommy guns and the drum magazines from his house. He spoke up. "Those drum magazines each hold a hunnerd forty-five caliber bullets and it's gonna take a while to load these drums. I called Guido to see if he would instruct us in shooting the three Tommy guns. He told me we would have to go to an outdoor shooting range because of the noise. He knows where one is and he'll go with us to use it."

"I let him know we didn't have any forty-five caliber bullets and he said he'd bring a big bunch," Tom informed them.

"By the way," Johnny said. "You Soldiers won't be shooting the Tommy guns when we go to war. But we still want you to learn how to shoot 'em."

The Soldiers were excited.

"We're gonna get more of 'em later. And you'll each have your own," Johnny told them.

Tom looked at his watch. "Say, Boss. We better get ready and go get Guido."

They had to use both of Johnny's and Tom's cars because of the guns. There would be seven shooters including Guido.

When they parked in front of Guido's store, Johnny and Tom went in to get him and the .45 caliber ammunition. The store owner was waiting for them. "Hey, guys. I got you a thousand rounds like Johnny wanted."

Johnny reached into his wallet. "You said it would be

ten boxes of a hunnerd bullets for fifty bucks." He pulled out five ten dollar bills. "The three of us can carry the boxes to my car."

Johnny and Guido got into his sedan with Charlie Diego, Eddie Edoardo and Rick Riccardo. Tom's Chevy Coupé had Gus in the little car as they went along the highways. The two cars went past the *Club Deluxe* after five miles then turned down a narrow road to an outdoor shooting range.

"Good!" Guido said. "There's no other shooters in the vicinity."

Everyone piled out of the cars and the Soldiers carried the three Tommy guns and the ammunition to a bench in the rear of the firing range. The first thing they did was to open up a couple of the bullet boxes.

"Give me your attention," Guido said. He took five bullets and inserted them into one of the drum magazines. "That's the way to load. Got it?" He put the loader in front of the trigger and pulled it a couple of times. With that demonstration done, he laid the weapon down on the bench.

Johnny picked Charlie Diego, Rick Riccardo and Guy Maglioni to begin putting bullets into the magazines.

"Okay," Guido said. "Listen to me. These weapons are called Thompson submachine guns, Tommy guns or Chicago typewriters. They are drum-fed as long as the triggers are pulled." He looked over at the loaders.

"Hold up. I want the other two drums pushed up into the lock in front of the triggers. Every one of you is going to take a gun and aim down to the target area."

Johnny, Tom and Gus each took one. Guido walked up behind them. He tapped them in order. They each quickly pulled the triggers. Next the loaders were rewarded for their work and they fired quickly. This was followed by the last who was Eddie Edoardo.

"At last!" he said as he pulled the trigger.

With that finished, they began loading, firing and reloading. Boss Johnny, Underboss Tom and Capo Gus did the most of the exercises since they were the ranking officers.

CHAPTER 18

Donna Sue and Sybil had made friends with the female cook Janet Meadows after accepting an invitation for coffee and cookies in the kitchen. Her husband Charlie along with the Mexican boys Manuel and Pedro had gone to the town of Waldo to pick up some grocery deliveries.

Dwayne and Pete went to Nigel Hawthorne's office to be briefed on the latest delivery of steel engravings. The Englishman ushered them into the engraving room where they were met by Fritz Harrigan.

He was all smiles. "Good morning, gentlemen!"

Hawthorne spoke up. "How is it going, Fritz old boy?"

Fritz pointed to a large stack of engravings wrapped in thick paper. "Those twenty-five are for Paraguay. The amount is one hundred Guarani. That's Jimmy Staunton's good work. They'll be divided in five packets for distribution when they arrive in South America."

Pete asked, "Exactly how are the engravings done?"

"Follow me," Fritz said. He led Dwayne and Pete to

where the engravers were working. There were five artists seated at their stations.

"The command station is where I work," Fritz said. "Right now things are going really well. We have various engraves, sculps and incises."

Pete looked over the workers' shoulders. "What are the mirrors in front of them for?"

"Ah!" Fritz said. "The mirrors that have been laid down for them is to see the bills backward. That way the engravers can look in the reflections since they have to reverse them. Printing them makes them be the right way when put on the paper."

"I get it," Pete said with a grin. "I was really confused there for a minute."

"My guys here each have a country to make their money," Fritz said. "It's Bolivian Bolivianos for Stanley, Chilean Pesos for Frank, Argentine Pesos for Robby, Guaranis for Jimmy and last but not least is Steve taking care of the Uruguay Peso. I pitch in when needed."

"I'm impressed," Dwayne said.

"I knew you would be," Hawthorne said. "Let's go back to my office. Rhodes is waiting to give you a complete tour of *The Headquarters*."

Herbert Rhodes nodded to them when they arrived outside Hawthorne's door. "I'll start with what things were used by the coders during the war. The most important thing was the running water being pumped up from the deep underground."

"I'm amazed," Pete said. "You'd think this was a desert from looking outside."

"There's complete plumbing through pipes in the building, sir. I'm sure you were able to get a drink of water, shave, and other such comforts this morning."

"Say!" Pete said. "And there is cold and hot water!"

"Right, sir. There is a rather large water heater in the back of the kitchen. That is where the petroleum truck drivers pump their gas inside. They show up twice a month. It's a welcome temperature around here when it's cold outside."

They followed him down to the barracks-like area. There were four guards sleeping and two were relaxing playing checkers.

"And we always have four guards on duty. Their monotony is broken on Tuesdays and Fridays."

Dwayne frowned. "What is that monotony?"

"That's their turn with the prostitutes, sir," Rhodes said.

"Oh, I see," Dwayne remarked.

"Certainly, sir," Rhodes said. "The engravers have Mondays and Thursdays. Wednesday is open for the officers."

"What about the whores?" Dwayne asked.

"There are five of them, sir. Quite clean and skillful. They were brought here from an expensive bordello in Mexico City. Their names are Alicia, Isabella, Valeria, Marta, and Panchita. Tomorrow is Wednesday. I'm sure we could arrange for you two to enjoy their talents. They are on the third floor if you're interested."

Dwayne grinned. "I don't think our wives would approve of that."

"Oh, yes," Rhodes stated. "You do have your wives with you, don't you?"

Pete laughed loudly. "Yes, we do and we want to be very careful."

"Of course, sir."

The next part of Rhode's tour took them from the deep basement, to the roof of the building, the cafeteria, second floor bedrooms and lastly the kitchen. When they walked in Donna Sue and Sybil were still there sitting around the table talking to Janet.

Rhodes said, "That is the tour, sirs. You'll have to excuse me now. I'll be seeing you later."

He walked out of the kitchen just as Janet's husband Charles Meadows appeared with some extra food he had ordered through the grocery store in Waldo. The Mexican boys Manuel and Pedro were with him.

"Hello, everybody," Charlie greeted. Then he looked at Janet. "We better start putting these in the freezer and the cabinets."

Janet said, "Our work starts. That's a hint, folks."

Dwayne and Donna Sue along with Pete and Sybil left the kitchen.

———

Two senior Treasury officers showed up in Wichita, Kansas' Municipal Airport in a mid-afternoon flight. After landing they walked into the building and looked around until they caught sight of the men who were supposed to meet them. These were Sam Ruggles A.K.A Treasury Agent-1 and Bob Turner A.K.A Treasury Agent-2.

Both were nervous about the arrivals since they were outranked by them. And at that moment, they didn't know where Dwayne Wheeler was. Ruggles and Turner shook hands with the arrivals.

"We can go downtown to where F.B.I. Agent Terry McCarthy has given us office space."

The two senior officers carried their own suitcases to the government car. Bob Turner opened the trunk so they could put their luggage in it. Everyone got into the automobile and Turner did the driving since he was the lowest ranking agent.

F.B.I. Agents Daniel Greenbern and George Taylor were still stiff from changing two flights to Wichita from Washington, D.C. They didn't say too much when they arrived at the 100 block of South Market where the WKH Building was.

Sam Ruggles got out and opened the trunk. He made sure he carried the two suitcases for the senior officers all by himself. Bob Turner headed for the parking garage used by people who worked in the WKH Building.

Ten minutes passed when Turner returned to Sam's and his office. He sat down and waited for the trouble to start.

"First thing," Daniel Greenbern said, "where is Dwayne Wheeler?"

"Uh...well, sir," Ruggles said. "At this moment we don't know."

"We had him driving trucks of cigarettes," Turner said. "But we told him to stop for a while."

"I see," Greenbern replied. "Can you explain that to us?"

"Yes, sir," Ruggles answered. "There has been some sort of war between the two cigarette forces."

"We have a bit of knowledge of that," Taylor said. "But what we don't know is how that situation brought about the trucks of cigarettes coming to a halt."

"The problem was in Panama City, sir," Turner told him. "They are not sending anything."

"Okay," Greenbern said. "We got that map Wheeler made for you. It shows three stops. Dallas, Wichita and Kansas City. There is no mention of the exact location of places where Panama City and New Orleans are staying. Nor does it give the location of Chicago."

"All that is true, sir," Ruggles said.

"We have a plan," Greenbern said. "It's a highly different sort of doing things for our department. The Treasury has given Taylor and me permission to use Elmer Pettibone and Jerry Owens along with Dwayne Wheeler to go from Wichita to Kansas City. That will get us closer to Chicago."

Sam Ruggles and Bob Turner exchanged surprised looks. "You know those guys?" Turner asked.

"Hell!" Taylor said. "We've known Pettibone for a hell of a long time. Wheeler and Owens are also old pals."

"We'll follow that map and the times on it," Greenbern said. "Pettibone and Owens will not be arrested."

Now Bob Turner spoke. "Isn't Wheeler going to be set free?"

"He's already free and has been for about seven months," George Taylor said.

"He doesn't have to be worried about being arrested for when he drove for another cigarette racket," Greenbern said. "It was when he was investigating that criminal Gilhooly woman and her sons that he was involved with those cigarettes. He also got into an outfit that strips down stolen cars and another that fences stolen goods."

Ruggles was flabbergasted. "He doesn't know that he's not wanted by the law?"

"Mmm," Greenbern said. "That'll be a happy surprise for Dwayne Wheeler!"

"He's gonna be enraged!" Ruggles said. "Turner and I have pulled him out of the private detective business."

"Okay," Greenbern said, "start calling his apartment telephone number tomorrow until he or his wife answers. What's her name?"

"Donna Sue," Ruggles said.

"In the meantime, George and I need a ride over to the Riverview Hotel," Greenbern stated.

"I'll take you to the parking garage for the ride," Turner said.

The three men left the building.

CHAPTER 19

I t was evening when Pete Van Dyke pulled up to the curb in front of the apartment house where Dwayne and Donna Sue lived. "Should I see you tomorrow, Pete?" Dwayne said.

"No," Pete said. "I'm pretty stiff from flying that C-37. Let's take a few days off."

They got their suitcases and made goodbyes. The couple went up the stairs and opened their apartment door. Dwayne set his suitcase down and went over to open the window.

"Whew! It got stuffy in here." He turned around and checked the doorjamb. It was still boarded up.

The couple went into the bedroom and began unpacking. Donna Sue gathered their clothes and divided them up between the cleaners and the laundry.

Dwayne looked over at Donna Sue. "D'you know what Fritz told me about Nigel Hawthorne and Herbert Rhodes."

"No. I don't know what Fritz told you about Nigel and Herbert."

"They both served in the British Army's Grenadier Guards."

"Well!" Donna Sue said. "I guess they talk about their experiences a lot, huh?"

"Not really," Dwayne said. "Nigel was kicked out of the outfit." He paused for a moment. "Y'know something. I ain't hungry after that flight."

"Me neither," she said. "Let's get under the shower and soap each other. Then I'll get us some fresh pajamas and we can get under those wonderful sheets and quilts."

It took them twenty minutes soaping each other down, drying and finally getting into bed. They dropped off to a long sleep in the bedroom.

———

EIGHT HOURS HAD PASSED WHEN THE PHONE rang. It woke them both up. Since the ringing was on Dwayne's side of the bed, he reached over and said a sleepy, "Hullo."

"Is that you, Dwayne?"

He sat up. "Yeah. Who're you?"

"I'm Sam Ruggles. And I got—"

"Who the hell is Sam Ruggles? I don't know you."

"Oh. You've known me as Treasury Agent-1."

Donna Sue looked over at Dwayne. "Who is the caller?"

Dwayne said, "It's that Treasury Agent-1 and says his name is Sam Ruggles." He spoke into the telephone. "How come you gave me your name, Ruggles?"

Ruggles was getting a little peeved. "That's my name, Dwayne! And Treasury Agent-2 is Bob Turner."

"What do you want?"

"This is going to be a big surprise for you," Ruggles

said. "There are some ranking agents by the name of Daniel Greenbern and George Taylor. We want you to come to Elmer Pettibone's warehouse."

Dwayne sat up straighter. "I want to know why I have to go over there! If you and those other guys have arrested him, then take 'em to the Sedgwick County Jail."

"We aren't going to arrest Pettibone," Ruggles said. "Jerry Owens and the old Walton brothers are here and they aren't getting arrested either. This is something big, understand?"

"Okay, I'll go over there then," Dwayne said.

Donna Sue got out of bed. "What in the world is going on?"

Dwayne hung up. "There's some Treasury agents over at Elmer Pettibone's. For some reason there's not gonna be any arrests." He got out of bed and headed for the closet. "I'll be goddamned if I'm gonna rush."

"I'll make us both some scrambled eggs and toast," Donna Sue said.

———

Johnny Forzini got Gus Augusto, Charlie Diego, Eddie Edoardo and Rick Riccardo in his Ford Sedan. Tom Lundari and Guy Magrione sat on the inside seat of his Chevy Coupé.

They were driving out to the submachine gun range to get some practice in. However, only Boss Johnny, Underboss Tom and Capo Gus would do any shooting with the Tommy guns. The Soldiers would fire the Beretta M1934 automatic pistols.

They turned off the highway and drove up on the trail to the targets. They reached the benches and stopped.

The Soldiers got out all the Tommy guns and Beretta ammunition.

The Tommy gun hundred drum magazines had been loaded the night before by the Soldiers. Now they were pushing bullets into the magazines of the pistols. Johnny had allowed each of them a Beretta model 1934.

Johnny inspected the drum magazines one more time. After that he gave the Soldiers enough time to load their pistols. When all was done, Johnny called everyone together.

"Okay, guys," he began, "it won't be long until we'll be laying in the dirt, aiming our guns at the cigarette truck coming our way. Me, Tom and Gus will be laying down with five paces between us. We'll have our ammo drums inserted properly and the safeties off. You Soldiers will lay with your pistols back of us. Any questions?"

The Soldiers shook their heads.

"When the truck is within range, me, Tom and Gus will start shooting our Tommy guns. As soon as the truck is stopped, all of us will jump up and attack the vehicle. That's when the Soldiers will shoot into the cab of the truck. Use one magazine then get rid of it and put another in. After that, don't shoot anymore! We don't want any ricochets hitting us."

The Soldiers nodded their heads affirmatively.

"After that we'll jump into our cars and head for Wichita. We have the map that shows us the exact location of those bastards' warehouse. If nobody is there, we'll hide out in the vicinity then attack. On the way Charlie Diego will reload my drum magazine, Eddie Edoardo will reload Capo Augusto's drum magazine and Guy Maglioni will reload Tom's drum magazine. You understand?"

"Don't worry, Boss," Charlie Diego assured him.

Johnny grinned. "We should get to Wichita in time to

shoot the place up. Then we can turn around and head back to Boston."

Guy Maglioni raised his hand. "What happens when we get back to Boston?"

"We begin taking over the city," Johnny said.

————

DWAYNE WHEELER DROVE UP TO ELMER Pettibone's warehouse and got out of his station wagon. He walked up to the entrance and put his ear against the door. He could hear the mumble of somebody talking. He opened the door and stepped inside and saw that everyone was seated near the armored truck.

"Ah ha! Here's our champion!" Elmer said.

Dwayne looked at Jerry Owens, Harry and Dennis Walton. Then he turned his eyes on the two guys Treasury Agent-1 and Treasury Agent-2. "What's your fucking names again?"

"I'm Sam Ruggles, Agent-1 and Bob Turner, Agent-2. You know us."

"I wasn't sure," Dwayne said and frowned at the next two.

"I'm Chief Daniel Greenbern. And this gentleman is Vice Chief George Taylor."

"Howdy," Dwayne said. "I'm happy about Elmer, Jerry and the Walton brothers not getting arrested. What brought that on?"

"You," Greenbern said.

"Me?"

"Yes, you. You weren't getting arrested for anything."

Dwayne snarled at Ruggles and Turner. "How come you two shitheads didn't tell me I wasn't going to be arrested."

"Forget it!" Greenbern said. "Here's what's going down. You and Jerry are going to follow the map that leads you to the warehouse in Kansas City. We'll be right behind you. Once we're inside there, we can get our hands on the map that leads the route out of Kansas City to Chicago."

"It'll work out well," Taylor said. "That's the last place in the operation. They'll be sitting around like Pettibone's outfit here. Panama City, New Orleans and Dallas can be taken care of. That is, if they are doing anything."

"Well," Dwayne said. "It's only a few days from this date." He turned his eyes on Ruggles and Turner. "I wish I could get my hands around your fucking necks!"

CHAPTER 20

Johnny Forzini's army was in its commander's ordered formation. They were stationed in a way that when the Wichita truck came over the hump it would be approximately 50 yards away on the dirt road.

Tom Lundari laid prone on the far left edge of their combat positions. He had his Tommy gun with the ammunition drum in place. Johnny was in the center with his Tommy gun the same way. Gus Augusto was on the right flank with his Tommy gun equally ready to fire on automatic.

Charlie Diego and Eddie Edoardo were positioned five or so yards in the rear between Tom and Johnny. Rick Riccardo and Guy Maglioni were settled in place between Tom and Gus.

Johnny raised up. "Remember, Soldiers! Do not shoot after Tom and Gus and me are shooting our Tommy guns and charging the truck. You might shoot one of us. So keep your safeties on those pistols. Understood?" He took a breath. "*Do you understand?*"

The four Soldiers gave affirmative replies.

———

DWAYNE AND JERRY WERE ROLLING ALONG slowly as the armored truck rocked back and forth on the rough road. Dwayne had his Colt .45 pistol in a shoulder holster and Jerry was holding on to his M1 semi-automatic rifle. The four treasury agents were in their official automobile rolling just a little more comfortably. Their position was behind the truck by several minutes.

Dwayne was driving and he felt a slight slide to the right and quickly turned the steering wheel. Immediately there was a sound of automatic weapons fire. There were some hits on the windshield coming from the front of the vehicle and rapid flashes ahead.

Dwayne hit the brakes and opened the armored door while drawing his pistol. Jerry had his rifle and immediately laid the weapon on the top of the door on his side. He aimed at two flashes and Dwayne aimed at one. Shots thundered from their guns.

All three automatics stopped.

There was the sound of running feet fading away. Dwayne and Jerry held their flashlights and moved slowly down the small draw. Three men with Tommy guns lay sprawled with bullet wounds. Two were obviously dead while one moaned. He was a muscular young man.

"Hey, shithead!" Dwayne said.

The man looked up at him, then his eyes stayed open and it was easy to see he had just died.

The sound of the agents' car came up and stopped. All four got out and looked in the illumination of the trucks' headlights. Greenbern was flabbergasted. "What the hell is this?"

"There was the sound of somebody running away," Jerry said. "Let's take a walk in that direction."

They went twenty yards and saw two automobiles. One was a 1941 Ford Sedan and the other a 1929 Chevy Coupé. There were footprints going past the vehicles.

"Man!" Dwayne said, chuckling. "I think those guys are 'fraidy cats."

"I wonder if this was from the Kansas City warehouse," George Turner said.

"Let's go back to see the stiffs," Dwayne remarked. "If they got car keys in their pockets, the others must be the down-and-out."

Dwayne walked over to one dead kid and knelt down. He felt around and pulled out some keys on a ring. He next walked over to the middle corpse and it was the same. The third that died the last only had apartment keys.

"Where's the nearest town?" Greenbern asked.

"I think if we drive on this road there'll be someplace civilized," Taylor said. "There's a roadmap in the glove compartment."

Bob Turner was chosen to look in the agents' car. "Yeah. Shawnee is the nearest town. We're still in Kansas." The treasury agents headed off to the town of Shawnee.

Dwayne and Jerry stayed at the site of the shootout. They climbed in the cab of the truck and got out their lunch buckets and thermoses.

Jerry said, "I'm sure glad I ain't going to jail."

Dwayne chuckled. "I'll bet Melanie will be, too. And so will Donna Sue." He took a drink of coffee. "Hey! I bet nobody told those poor bastards that the trucks were armored. Let's get these three Tommy guns laying by them dead guys. I'll bet there's ammo in those two cars! We can take 'em back to Wichita!"

"For some reason I think that's a fine idea," Jerry said with a wide grin.

The two laid their lunches down and jumped out of

the cab. Dwayne picked up two of the Tommy guns while Jerry secured the Tommy gun that belonged to the muscular kid. Next they went to the two cars and found ten boxes of .45 caliber ammunition in the Ford Sedan.

They carried everything back to the truck and shoved the guns and ammo under the seats. Dwayne climbed in and sat in the driver's side. Jerry took the passenger's position and reached into the glove compartment for the map.

"Okay, Dwayne, we don't want to run into them agents," he said. "So this map shows we can skirt around them if we get on to U.S. 50."

"Let me see the map. Right! Go through Newton, then turn south to Wichita on U.S. 81."

Dwayne backed up and turned to the rear. After going ten miles he turned down a county road to U.S. 50. They reached the highway then settled in for a nice drive south to Wichita.

Jerry was quiet for a while then he remarked, "Dwayne, what are we gonna do with them guns and ammo?"

"Mmm," Dwayne mused. "I hadn't thought of that."

Jerry shrugged. "Since I ain't gonna get thrown in jail, I'll be going back to driving a taxi. Do you want all them guns?"

"Well, I'm a private detective, so I might really need some of that stuff."

"I'll just keep my M-1 rifle."

"Well, when we get back to Wichita I'll hide the Tommy guns and all the drums and ammo."

"Have you got a good place to hide all that stuff?" Jerry asked.

"I sure do," he said.

"It's as simple as that, ain't it?"

"Sure," Dwayne said. "Are you sure you don't want any of this war stuff?"

"I prefer driving a taxi, Dwayne," Jerry said, clearing his throat. "Why don't us four go to the Stockyard Restaurant tomorrow?"

"That's a damn fine idea, Jerry."

CHAPTER 21

Dwayne and Jerry didn't waste any time in driving from the scene of the battle back to Wichita. They went as fast as the armored truck would go.

The two reached the city and in a short time they sighted the door of the warehouse. They pulled up to it and honked several times. The door was pushed open by elderly Dennis Walton. Elmer Pettibone followed as Dwayne drove across the wide floor and parked.

"What happened, guys?" Elmer said. He and the Walton brothers were curious.

"We got ambushed by some dickheads that evidently didn't know the truck was armored," Dwayne informed him.

Elmer turned his attention to Jerry. "Since we didn't get thrown into the Sedgewick County slammer, I've been waiting to talk to you. You used to drive a taxi here in Wichita, right?"

"Right."

"Well, how'd you like to see this warehouse get some cabs in here. I'm talking about driving for the public."

Dwayne patted Jerry on the shoulder. "Sure! And think of how happy Melanie will be."

"Hey, yeah!" Jerry said. He turned to look at Elmer. "Are you serious?"

"Hey, I got the dough scattered around. No problem!" He looked at Harry and Dennis. "These guys are gonna be the mechanics."

"You bet!" Harry said as Dennis nodded his head.

"I'm gonna close my Roadhouse just for a celebration," Elmer said. "I want Dwayne and Donna Sue, Jerry and Melanie and these good ol' guys Harry and Dennis. That'll be tomorrow evening."

"Great," Jerry said. He looked over at Dwayne. "C'mon, I'll help you take that stuff out of the cigarette truck."

The two pair walked over to the armored vehicle. Jerry helped Dwayne carry the submachine guns and ammo over to his car. With the chore done, both men shook hands and got into their personal autos.

Dwayne drove out of the warehouse and turned down Market to Douglas then another turn to drive to the garage. When he reached his parking place, he looked around to make sure there was nobody else nearby. With that done, he pulled out the weaponry. It was heavy in the small satchel, but he managed to get it over to his apartment.

Donna Sue greeted him and gave him a big, loving kiss.

"Hey," he said. "I'm gonna have to pry the other doorjamb open. C'mon in the bedroom." He carried the suitcase and laid it on the bed. He opened it up and stepped back. "How d'you like that?"

"Where did you get those things?"

"In a battle, baby," Dwayne said. "We were fired on

first. The poor stupid kids didn't know the truck was an armored 1.5-ton model. They fired on us, and me and Jerry shot back and it didn't take long to kill 'em. Only a quick ten seconds. These are Tommy guns. Three of 'em!"

"What are those round things?" Donna Sue asked.

"Those are type 'C' drum magazines. They each hold a hundred .45 caliber bullets."

"What are you going to do with all that, Dwayne?

"I already told you. I'm gonna put 'em in the empty doorjamb," he said taking off his jacket. "If there's a need for 'em I'll be ready. Who knows? I might need a weapon that fires 700 to 800 rounds a minute."

"Get rid of them, Dwayne!"

"Hell no! I got these from some shitheads who tried to kill me and Jerry."

"It's a good thing this apartment belongs to us," Donna Sue pouted.

"It sure is. I gotta go get a number 6 jimmy." He hurried to the kitchen and pulled his tool chest out from under the sink. When he got back he took the jimmy and gently pried down the doorjamb on one side, being careful not to spoil the paint or the wood.

"Dwayne, I don't like what you're doing!"

He stopped. "Looky here, Donna Sue. I want these Tommy guns and drums. And I'm gonna put 'em in this doorjamb."

"Won't those doorjambs crash with all that stuff?"

Dwayne frowned. "Them doorjambs are what's holding up the ceiling."

He turned to the chore and pulled the side off and carefully put the drum magazines on top of the other. Next came the Tommy guns put in side-by-side.

"There they are," Dwayne said. He put the slat of the doorjamb back. Nothing revealed the contents. He turned to Donna Sue. "I've got some good news for you. D'you want to go to Elmer's Roadhouse tomorrow evening? There'll be Elmer Pettibone and his wife Jewel, Jerry Owens and Melanie, the old Walton brothers, and you and me. Elmer's going to pay the bill. And it'll be a big one."

"I'm not surprised."

"Say, I almost forgot," Dwayne said. "Elmer is going to build up a taxi company."

"Well, he's got the money. And the brains."

———

Dwayne and Donna Sue walked across the parking area of the Roadhouse. Jack Wallace and Denny Tarbal, the bouncers, greeted them. "Have fun, you guys. It's all for you."

They entered and spotted Mr. and Mrs. Elmer Pettibone sitting at the table with the Walton brothers. Dwayne waved and he and Donna Sue joined them. They just sat down when Jerry and Melanie showed up.

"Okay!" Elmer said. He turned his head and hollered for service. "We're ready to eat!"

"Yes, sir," his waiter said.

He passed eight menus out then asked for their drinks. It was an even break of red wine between the married people but the two Walton brothers chose beer. The waiter came back with the drinks then took the orders for the main courses. It was salads and the Roadhouse's delicious steaks and fried potatoes.

As the meal was being eaten, Elmer did all the talking. "I didn't do this for eating alone. I wanted to discuss the taxi business I'm planning on creating. First thing is getting the funds, right? Right! I got enough money scattered between here and foreign banks not to have to get any loans, right? Right! I'm starting with people I trust. That'd be Jerry as the chief taxi driver while Harry and Dennis will work the mechanical side, right? Right!" He looked over at Dwayne. "And if I ever need a private detective I'll call you, right?"

"Right!" Dwayne replied.

Elmer laughed. "Okay! He picked up his wine and said, "I want to toast my new employees." Glasses were raised and clinked. Elmer looked over at Dwayne. "And here's to the best goddamn driver I ever had. Dwayne Wheeler!" Another toast followed.

"Okay," Elmer said. "Anybody for dessert?"

DWAYNE WAS SEATED AT THEIR BREAKFAST table with Donna Sue when the phone rang. She got up and went over to answer. "Hello. Yes, he is."

"Who is it?"

"One of those Treasury agents."

"Aw, shit!" Dwayne said. He took the phone from Donna Sue. "Yeah? Who is this?"

"This is Sam Ruggles. Bring those submachine guns back."

"What submarines?"

"Not submarines, God damn it! Submachine guns! The ones that were laying in the mud by those dead guys you and Owens killed."

"We didn't do anything with 'em. After you guys left, we came straight back to Wichita. We didn't think of taking 'em with us."

"That's a lot of bullshit," Ruggles said. "And if you guys got 'em you'd better give 'em up."

"Look! After me and Jerry left, there was a chance for gangsters to come and pick up the weapons. That is the only thing I can think could happen."

"I'm giving you orders right now; don't leave your house!"

"I live in an apartment."

"*Stay at that apartment then!* Bob Turner is going over to search you and your buddy's house or apartment or whatever. He's on his way!"

CHAPTER 22

On the day that Agents Sam Ruggles and Bob Turner searched for the Tommy guns they were unable to find the weapons. Two women—Donna Sue Wheeler and Melanie Owens—were livid. The rowdy Treasury Agents searched their dwellings in a rough manner that tore up every room, pieces of furniture, kitchenware, picture frames, luggage, bathrooms, etc.

Then they left without cleaning the mess up.

A complaint was made by Dwayne Wheeler and Jerry Owens through attorney Carl Banter of Wichita, Kansas. The lawyer wrote a fiery letter to the Treasury in Washington with photographs attached.

A return answer of the Treasury in Washington replied that Treasury Agents Sam Ruggles and Bob Turner had been transferred to Greenland. Banter advised Dwayne and Jerry to forget the problem. It would cost them a lot of trouble.

———

TWO WEEKS PASSED WHEN DWAYNE WHEELER and Peter Van Dyke had to make another flight from Wichita to *The Headquarters*. Both Donna Sue and Sybil would be holding down the fort while their husbands were gone. The ladies were going to enjoy being on the top floor of the Riverside Hotel. They wrote down a lot of suggestions for their next shopping trip. Donna Sue suggested Oklahoma City and Sybil seconded the proposition.

While the women were concentrating on their happy days to come, Dwayne drove his Nash station wagon out to the airport with Pete as a passenger. He parked in the tarmacs for aviators and he and Pete hurried over to the C-37 airplane rentals.

They took off and soared up to Pete's desired altitude. He glanced over at Dwayne and yelled, "How'd you like to do a bit of piloting?"

"Sure," Dwayne shouted. "But if I go crazy and let loose of the yoke, you take over."

"You betcha," Pete assured him loudly.

Then Dwayne practiced with the yoke gradually, eventually feeling easy with the aerial maneuvers. Pete also let him go back and forth in complete turns.

"How's that?" Dwayne asked.

"Damned good, I'm not kidding. The next time we go up, I can give you more lessons." He settled down on the beam toward the destination.

Ninety minutes later Pete landed the Cessna C-37 and taxied up to the entrance of *The Headquarters*. Nigel Hawthorne and Herbert Rhodes were standing in front of the door and were glad to see them. They walked up to the airplane when the propeller stopped spinning.

"Good news!" Nigel said. "We've got enough engravings for all our customers."

"Wow," Pete said. "I knew we were doing good but not that good." He looked behind Nigel. The six engravers were standing tall and happy, waving at them.

Nigel spoke up. "We're going to have to fly back to Wichita for a meeting with the South Americans. There are six flying into America. I know there are five nations but I don't know who is who. There is also an Argentine Army officer coming along with them. He's a paratrooper commander and is going to lead the attack in the mountains."

"I bet he's a tough guy," Pete said.

"You're right about that," Dwayne agreed. He stretched. "All we got to do is fill up the tank and fly back to Wichita."

When the C-37 was refueled, Nigel put his luggage on the plane to fly to Wichita. Rhodes and the engravers waved happy goodbyes as Peter Van Dyke lifted off the ground.

———

PETE LANDED THE PLANE IN THE DARK EXCEPT for the runway lights. He turned off the engine and the trio stepped down on the tarmac. "I'll turn in the plane and join you over at Dwayne's station wagon."

When Pete was finished, Dwayne drove over to the Riverview Hotel. When he reached downtown he stopped to let Pete and Nigel out. They went into the lobby and walked over to Paul Tracey, the night receptionist.

"There are six South Americans showing up here," Pete said. "Keep 'em all on the second floor."

Dwayne drove over to his parking lot and grabbed his suitcase then headed for the apartment house. When he knocked and walked in, Donna Sue was sitting on the sofa in her housecoat. She also had a bowl of popcorn in her lap.

"Hey! You're back early!"

"Yeah," Dwayne said. "There was a change. A good change! The South Americans are due to fly into Wichita in a couple of days. I thought there was five of 'em but it looks like there was six." He took off his jacket and put it in the hall closet then walked back and joined her on the sofa. "By the way, it looks like all the work we were doing in *The Headquarters* is finished."

"Well, little boy, you just be nice and I'll pour you some Jack Daniels as a reward," Donna Sue said. She started for the kitchen, then stopped and turned. "Don't touch any of that popcorn, okay?"

"Can't I have *any* popcorn?"

"Okay, you can have *some* popcorn. So! What do you want first? Jack Daniels or popcorn?"

"Jack Daniels, please."

———

THE SOUTH AMERICAN CONTINGENT SHOWED UP at the Wichita Municipal Airport late in the afternoon. Peter Van Dyke, Nigel Hawthorne and Dwayne Wheeler met them with three automobiles from the Riverside Hotel. The eight people crowded into the vehicles while the Hotel Riverview bellboys put all the luggage in the trunks, then got into the driver sides of the seats.

The convoy headed out from the airport and drove straight to the hotel. It pulled up in front and the bellboys immediately got out of the cars and took the luggage into the lobby. Pete, Dwayne and Nigel stood by.

The hotel manager Charles Bentley stood at the front side of the desk greeting the six South Americans while the two receptionists Darrell Crawley and Paul Tracey began getting their names.

The next step was the South Americans going up to the second floor to their assigned rooms of two each. However, there was a Colonel Martin who had a room all his own.

Jimmy Thompson, the bell captain, went upstairs and announced that dinner was being served in the hotel's dining room.

THE NEXT MORNING THE HOTEL AUDITORIUM was prepared for the South Americans and the American staff. A breakfast was laid out with the cooks serving a choice of food for everyone including the three Americans.

There was a lot of busy Spanish-speaking during the eating of eggs cooked as desired, bacon, sausages, different rolls, toast, biscuits, jelly, butter, fruit, coffee, and tea. The guests were in no hurry as they leisurely consumed the sustenance. Dwayne, Pete and Nigel were irritated by the slowness, but they were under orders to let the South Americans go at their own pace.

Finally, after two hours, the diners waited for the waiters to clear the tables. Pete got to his feet. "My name is Peter Van Dyke. I am pleased to welcome our guests. Our victory is near."

There was applause from the South Americans.

Pete introduced, "Dwayne Wheeler and Nigel Hawthorne."

Both men stood up and were given more applause.

"Now," Pete said. "If you please, I want you to let us know who you are and your nationality."

"Of course," the leading South American said. "My name is Juan Garcia from Argentina."

The next was, "I am called Alonso Miguel from Chile."

"I am Federico Serrano from Argentina."

"I am Carlos Ortiz from Paraguay."

"I call myself León Castro from Bolivia."

"Alfredo Torres from Uruguay."

"I am Colonel Vicente Martin of the Argentine Army Paratroopers."

"Excellent!" Pete said. "You must forgive us Americans for not knowing any Spanish."

Juan Garcia spoke politely. "You need not forgive us, Mister Van Dyke. We all speak English, and the aid you have given our nations is more than enough."

"Thank you, Mister Garcia," Pete said. "We were told that you would know about the planned attack on the Nazis."

"Indeed," Garcia said. "For that I will turn you over to Colonel Martin."

The paratrooper officer stood up with official military reports in his hands. He was in a civilian suit, but he still had a military appearance. "I am happy to be in this operation. We are going to have it easy to defeat the Nazis. Their headquarters are in a valley of the Cristal de Roca Mountains. The location is close to the Aconcagua range which has an elevation of 22,837 feet. However, that is no problem since we airborne troops will make a parachute jump into the Cristal de Roca Mountains where the Nazis are located. That drop will be 600 feet high."

Dwayne raised his hand. "That's kind of low, isn't it?"

"Yes," Colonel Martin said. "But it cannot be helped. The Nazis have a strong log fortress on the drop zone.

When the parachutists have landed they will make an upward attack through the snow."

Once again Dwayne raised his hand. "Won't it be a long time to wait for winter?"

"No," Colonel Martin said, being polite. "Argentina is in the lower hemisphere while the United States is in the higher. Argentina's winter is in the United States' summer." He paused. "American children receive their Christmas presents while it is quite cold and Argentine children receive their presents while it's quite warm. That is all done at the same time. Thus the Argentine para-troops are cold this time of the year."

"Well, I'll be damned," Dwayne said with a smile. "I'm glad you told me that."

"I'm glad, too," Colonel Martin said. He cleared his throat. "Now. There will be two C-47s of the *Argentine Fuerza Aérea*. Excuse me, I meant to say the Argentine Air Force. Each aircraft will have a two-man 60-milimeter mortar team who will have Colt pistols. The other twenty men will be riflemen with the American Army's M-1. Thus we have forty-two men, two mortars, two Colt pistols and forty rifles."

Pete and Nigel were writing down the military information.

"We had a spy in the log fortress for about eight months before he made a planned escape," the colonel said. "He made sketches, marked out gun positions and offices, barracks and an engraving studio." He smiled. "Nazi engraving of money was very poor. You can congratulate your artists in *The Headquarters* that their work will be permanent and put into legal tender." He folded his report. "*Ya es término!*"

The entire room of three Americans and seven South Americans broke into cheers.

CHAPTER 23

The next day Dwayne Wheeler, Peter Van Dyke and Nigel Hawthorne were sitting in the coffee shop of the Riverside Hotel. The trio was not speaking much as they ate their breakfasts. Dwayne took a sip of coffee then set his cup down.

"Y'know, guys. All last night I was thinking about something. And the more I thought about it, the more I wanted to do it."

Pete looked over at him. "You're not going to ask Donna Sue for a divorce, are you?"

"No. She would kill me and take charge of the Dwayne Wheeler Detective Agency if I did that."

"Well then, old boy," Nigel said, "what were you thinking of?"

"You guys are going to think I'm crazy."

Pete shrugged. "If you want the truth, we do indeed know you're crazy."

"Spill it," Nigel said.

"I'd like to go down to South America and jump with

Colonel Martin's parachute regiment when he attacks those Nazis."

"Are you kidding?" Pete said. He didn't speak for a moment. "On the other hand, that might be fun. You know what I mean? One last adventure before we get in the old rocking chairs." He looked at Nigel. "What do you think?"

"Good God no!" Nigel said. "I heard about too many failed parachutes after D-Day."

"That wasn't failed parachutes," Dwayne said. "It was the gliders that killed the most of our soldiers."

"So what?" Nigel said.

Pete turned and looked at, Dwayne. "Are you serious about this?"

"Well...damn it! I am serious. Let's go and talk to Colonel Martin about it."

Dwayne stood up and looked at Nigel. "Are you sure you don't want to go with us?"

"You're damn right I'm sure I don't want to go with you chaps. If God wanted to let people jump from high places, he would have given them wings."

Dwayne and Pete left the coffee shop and went up to the second floor in the elevator. They walked down the hall to Colonel Martin's room. Pete knocked on the door.

The paratrooper appeared. "Please come in. What can I do for you?"

The two Americans saw that he had called up room service for his breakfast.

"Good morning, Colonel," Pete said. "We would like to ask a favor of you."

"Certainly."

"We, that is, Dwayne and I would like to go down to Argentina and make a parachute jump with your regiment in the attack on the log fortress."

"Ah, so you are both ex-paratroopers, eh?"

"Actually," Dwayne said, "we're *not*. But we'd like to go along just the same."

"Mmm," said Colonel Martin.

"I guess we would be trained on how to jump out of an airplane."

Pete spoke up. "We are fast learners. And we were with each other in the European War."

"Uh..." the colonel said, "we have got to go in two weeks. That is not the usual amount of training for parachutists." He thought a moment. "I have a *suboficial mayor* who speaks English. He could teach you how to leap from a flying aircraft."

"What is a *subo-er*, a *subo-er*..." stuttered Dwayne.

"A *suboficial mayor* is a chief warrant officer," Colonel Martin said. "But I must warn you he is a tough teacher."

"That's not a problem," Pete said. "Dwayne and I were in the military police."

"Then I have no objection," the Colonel told him. "But I am flying to Argentina tomorrow. You should come with me or you have no chance to learn how to make a jump. My flight is at ten a.m. Then it is three other flight changes."

"We'll buy our tickets to go with you," Pete said.

Dwayne said, "We need to buy paratroop boots and warm field military uniforms. There's an excellent Army Surplus Store here in Wichita."

"We can provide you with uniforms, but you'll have to get your own jump boots."

"C'mon, Pete!" Dwayne said. "Let's go buy the boots at the Army Surplus Store. It's around the corner."

"I'm right behind you."

The two Americans left the room and Colonel Martin

set down to his breakfast. He took a sip of hot coffee and wondered if he had made a mistake.

———

THE WIVES OF DWAYNE AND PETE WERE surprised that their husbands had been ordered to South America. They were not happy about not being able to go with them, but knew the trip was a top secret activity.

———

THE TWO AMERICANS TRAVELED WITH COLONEL Vicente Martin for a total of twenty-four hours in three changes of flight before getting to the *Estación de Paracaídas*. There was snow on the ground and a command car was waiting for Colonel Martin. When they reached his headquarters, Martin sent for *Suboficial Mayor* Ignacio Platas.

The warrant officer presented himself ten minutes later. He showed a snappy salute and said, "*Estoy aquí, mi Coronel.*" He was a bit taken aback by the two Americans.

Colonel Martin said, "We can speak English, Chief Warrant Officer Platas."

"Yes, my Colonel."

"They are here to go with us on the operation in the mountains," Colonel Martin said. "You are ordered to get them the equipment, uniforms and rifles they will need."

"Yes, my Colonel."

"And you must instruct them on how to jump with parachutes."

"Excuse me, my Colonel. Did you say I have to teach them how to be parachutists?"

"Yes, Chief Warrant Officer Platas. You may begin your instructions as quickly as possible."

Platas saluted then turned to Dwayne and Pete. "Come with me."

He led them out the door. "May I know your names?"

"Of course. I am Dwayne Wheeler."

"And I am Peter Van Dyke."

"Are you in the military?"

"Oh, no, Pete said. "But my friend and I were in the military police in the war in Europe."

"I see," the Chief Warrant Officer said, grimacing. "Well, I'll take you to the officers' quarters first."

It was cold as he led them to the officers' billet and took them inside. A paratrooper was seated at a desk and he and the Chief Warrant Officer exchanged a short conversation in Spanish.

"There is an empty quarters for you to use," Platas said. They went down the hallway and Platas opened the door. "You can put your suitcases in here. Now we will go to the quartermaster."

Once more the Chief Warrant Officer escorted the two Americans across the garrison. This time it was to draw their combat clothing. Platas spoke in rapid Spanish and the clerk followed his orders. Two of everything was put on the counter: field jackets, field trousers, fatigue shirts and trousers, woolen stocking caps, socks, and gloves.

"The last items are duffel bags," Platas said. "You can stuff the clothes in the duffel bags as ordered."

Dwayne and Pete gathered it all up and were marched back to the officers' quarters.

They went down the hall and opened the door. Bedding was now on the bunks and a small chair and desk were against the far wall. Platas sat down in the chair and spoke.

"Get dressed!"

As Dwayne and Pete followed his orders, the Chief Warrant Officer noticed their muscularity. When the two dressed in the uniforms and put on the jump boots purchased in Wichita, they left the quarters and were taken over to the warehouse.

The items they drew there were a rucksack, weapons case, ammo belt, helmet, canteen and holder. Once more Platas marched them back to the quarters. "All right! Take off your woolen stocking caps and put on your helmets. Then *Outside*!"

The two were marched over to the jump school area. "Now!" said a friendlier Chief Warrant Officer. "The type of parachute you will jump with is the U.S. Army T-5's. But first, you must learn how to keep from breaking your legs."

They were taken to a place where several 4-foot platforms were standing. "I am going to teach you how to do the Parachute Landing Fall also called a P.L.F. I got my parachute training in Fort Benning, Georgia in the U.S. Army. So! I am going to get up on that 4-foot platform and perform a side P.L.F."

He got up on the platform and shouted the order. "Ready! Prepare to land! *Land*!"

He jumped straight away from the platform and performed a side landing.

"Okay. I want you to perform a P.L.F."

Dwayne did the first attempt and was followed by Pete.

Chief Warrant Officer Platas was pleased. "That is pretty good. So let's try other directions."

He took them through front, sides and rear P.L.F.s.

The next few days were spent on exiting from an aircraft. They also ran along with a platoon of Argentine paratroopers every morning to get in shape. Dwayne and Pete sweated under the uniform and were breathing hard after each run. The one good thing was the officer's mess where the food was good.

On the final night before the attack, the two Americans stayed in their quarters and didn't talk very much after they were issued two American M-1 rifles.

CHAPTER 24

The first C-47 in the aerial attack was closing in to drop the paratroopers it carried. Dwayne and Pete were the last in the stick. Colonel Martin placed them there in case they were too afraid to jump out of the aircraft.

All the jumpers were feeling the cold as the airplane lumbered through the air. The jumpmaster, a *teniente*, was standing in the door looking out over the snow 900 feet down.

There was a red and green light at the side of the door. It was red, then suddenly green. The jumpmaster went out the door and the paratroopers were right behind him. Dwayne went out in the proper position as Chief Warrant Officer Platas taught them. He counted loudly, "*Hut-thousand! two-thousand! three-thousand! four-thousand!*"

Suddenly he was jerked so hard that his helmet slipped on his head. He pushed the headgear back and looked around. Then he made an excellent left side P.L.F. He got to his feet and undid his harness and weapons case. He had to open the latter and pull the M1 rifle out.

"Hey, Parachutist!"

Dwayne saw Pete struggling through the snow toward him. "Hey, yourself, Parachutist."

They moved fast toward Colonel Vicente Martin. Members of his staff were around him. He used his binoculars to scan the log fortress. One of the 60-millimeter mortars was quickly set up next to him. He guessed the range and the mortar man dropped a shell down the tube. It was launched by an expert.

The shell hit the front of the fortress and the blast sent some of the logs flying. The mortar man got ready to drop another shell, but the Colonel stopped him.

"White flag!" he said. Then the call of "cease fire" ran through the paratroopers group. They all held their weapons without moving.

The colonel looked around for Dwayne and Pete. He signaled them to join him. The commanding officer, his adjutant and the two Americans moved as fast as possible through the knee deep snow.

The people in the log fortress came out holding their hands high. "*Suspender el fuego*! *Sich ergeben*! We surrender!"

The paratroopers formed up and moved carefully toward the Nazis. More appeared with their hands over their heads. Colonel Vicente ordered a *capitán* to take some paratroopers inside and search the interior of the fortress.

Meanwhile the colonel finally met the Nazi commander Heinrich Stark. His Spanish wasn't very good but he was fluent in English. "We're lost. Just lost."

Colonel Martin signaled to Dwayne and Pete to join them. "Gentlemen," he said. "These are the Nazis who failed."

"What went wrong for you?" Dwayne said.

"It was our engravers," the Nazi said. "Their work was so terrible that we could not pass the money. We didn't know who the expert engravers were. Therefore, we couldn't hunt them down."

"Well, you're looking at Dwayne Wheeler and Peter Van Dyke," Colonel Martin said. "And that's all I'm going to tell you."

The Nazi was amazed. "Aren't they paratroopers?"

Colonel Martin laughed aloud. "Hell, yes, they're paratroopers. And damn good ones, too."

Dwayne and Pete grinned at each other.

———

DWAYNE AND PETE GOT BACK TO WICHITA three days later at ten o'clock in the morning. Their wives met them at the Municipal Airport building and both men were happy to be home. They were horny, but they were also going to show their wives something really "neat."

"Can't you show us now?" Donna Sue asked.

"Nope," Dwayne said.

Pete said, "You gals are gonna really be impressed."

The couples made plans to meet at the Stockyards Restaurant that evening at eight o'clock. Donna Sue drove their Nash station wagon and parked at their usual place. Dwayne opened the back of the vehicle and pulled his suitcase and duffel bag out.

"What's that?" Donna Sue asked.

"Oh, some army stuff."

"Hey, Dwayne! Don't start getting smart with me. What is this 'neat' thing you're crowing about."

"Not to worry."

They walked over to their apartment house and went

upstairs. He got the duffel bag and called to Donna Sue. "Do you want to see the duffel bag stuff?"

"Sure," she said. "But I hope it's not more submachine guns."

He opened up the duffel bag and began pulling out items. "We were at an Argentine Army base. They gave us a field jacket, field trousers, fatigue shirts and regular trousers, woolen stocking caps, socks, and gloves. It was snowing and really cold." He paused. "Did you know that there's the top of the world and the bottom. They have a different climate. Summer is warm in our climate and theirs is cold. So you can see..."

"Of course I know that," Donna Sue said. She put the woolen stocking cap on. "Don't I look cute?"

"Yes, you do."

"By the way. What is that something *real neat* you and Pete are going to show us? I hate to have something I can't see. Or pick up. Or kick!"

"Patience, little one."

Donna Sue pushed the woolen stocking cap forward over her forehead. "I may be not in the mood to go into the bedroom."

"Oh, yeah?" Dwayne said. He scooped her up and walked across the apartment to drop her on the bed.

She jumped up and said, "I guess I better get out of my clothes, huh?"

"That's it, kid."

———

DWAYNE AND DONNA SUE WERE A TRIFLE AHEAD of Pete and Sybil going into the Stockyard Restaurant parking area. They teamed up—men with men and women with women—and headed for the door. The maître d' took the couples to a table for four and seated them. "The waiter will be with you shortly."

Sybil looked over at Donna Sue. "Pete won't tell me what him and Dwayne are going to show us."

Pete grinned. "You'll see that it's something very, very wonderful."

"Wonderful?" Sybil said. "I've never heard you say that word before."

The wine master took their order and quickly came back with it. He opened the bottle and asked, "Which of the following gentleman wishes to be the taster?"

"You be it, Pete," Dwayne suggested.

Pete had an excellent taste for wines. He smelled the glass, swished it, sipped it, and pronounced it superlative. The wine was poured by the wine master then the waiter walked up.

"Have you decided on the salad?"

All chose a Caesar. Then the usual Stockyard meal of sirloin medium-well, baked potatoes, and green beans was requested. When all was on the table, the eating commenced. That took a half hour; then there was the dessert of chocolate soufflé. That was another twenty minutes of eating.

"Now! What is this thing you have promised us?" Donna Sue said.

"Yes!" Sybil said. "What is this *wonderful* item?"

Both men reached into their inside coat pockets. They pulled the objects out and showed them. The women were not impressed. "What are those?"

"Look," said Dwayne. "Both of 'em are metal wing insignias. They're two inches long."

The women squinted their eyes and weren't impressed a bit.

"Damn it!" Pete growled. "Can't you two see what's

on the wings? There are parachutes. And look at the arch over it. It says **PARACAIDISTA MILITAR**."

"It's in Spanish!" Dwayne said.

Sybil said, "I don't know Spanish!"

"I don't either," Donna Sue echoed.

Pete looked at Dwayne, then looked at both women. "That means 'military parachutist.' We were decorated with these wings because we made a military parachute jump in Argentina."

There was a quiet moment, then both women let out feminine shrieks in unison. "Don't ever do that again!"

The waiter came over. "Is everything all right?"

Donna Sue glowered at him. "*No! Nothing is all right!*"

CHAPTER 25

When the Johnson County Sheriff and the Federal agents went to the site of the battle, they found foot prints of four or five individuals running like hell deeper into Missouri.

———

EVENTUALLY THE INFORMATION OF JOHNNY Forzini, Tom Lundari and Gus Augusto was sent to the Boston police, who sent out officers to inform the families. The relatives of the dead were given strenuous questioning by not only the Boston police but also the F.B.I. The latter was looking to see if the Mafia was coming back. The girls Sofia Vanacore and Maria Palma were accused of being young prostitutes and gun molls.

The Boston neighborhood where Johnny Forzini, Tom Lundari and Gus Augusto had lived was bewildered and frightened. They didn't know their youths' corpses had been kept in a morgue in Shawnee, Kansas. However, they had been given autopsy reports to read.

Charlie Diego, Eddie Edoardo, Rick Riccardo and Guy Maglioni managed to run due north. They had the money that Johnny had given them. It was enough for them to buy bus tickets and return to their homes. When they arrived at their neighborhood they went straight to old Carlo Tedeschi.

The owner of the Ristorante Italiana was startled to see the four young guys. "Are the rest of your pals dead?"

"You bet your ass they're dead," Charlie Diego said bitterly. "We was laying behind them and suddenly Johnny, Tom and Gus started shooting. They didn't get many shots at the truck we were laying for. Then there was guys shooting from the truck. Them two killed our buddies!"

Guy Maglioni was angry. "The fucking battle wasn't worth a thing."

Rick Riccardo whined. "We didn't even know where we was once we started running."

"Okay," the old man said. "You guys got former jobs, right?"

"Sure," Rick Diego said. "I was working at Giovonni's Filling Station."

"We worked at the Sereno Bakery," Eddie Edoardo said. He nodded to Guy Maglioni. "That's right."

Charlie Diego said, "I was a janitor in the Conforto Building. But I'm pretty certain I can get my job back."

"Okay," Carlo said. "I'll go see what I can do. But I may have to give somebody a dishwashing job."

———

DWAYNE WHEELER, PETER VAN DYKE, NIGEL Hawthorne and Herbert Rhodes stood together in front of *The Headquarters*. The building was empty. A quartermaster major had come to remove all the U.S. Army's property that was usable. His soldiers put seven loads in the backs of two-and-a-half ton trucks. With that done, a transport company of drivers hopped in the cabs and started off for Fort Riley, Kansas.

When the last truck was driven past Dwayne, Pete, Nigel and Herbert, they walked into the building to look around. They went to the kitchen and saw that Charlie Meadows with his wife Janet and the two Mexican boys had left a clean area.

Pete chuckled. "I guess cooks and kitchen workers hate to leave any grime."

Dwayne shrugged. "The floor is gonna be blasted to hell, yet look at it. It's been mopped."

Herbert Rhodes slowly walked down the hallway with the others behind him. "Here's where our engravers worked." He looked at Dwayne. "Did you say the Krauts weren't very good at that art?"

"Yeah," Dwayne replied. "They were really inept. The best of our guys was Fritz Harrigan. He was a Wichita boy. I wonder what he's gonna do now."

"He'll find something, believe me."

"I'll never forget that parachute jump," Pete said. "What about you, Dwayne?"

"It was really something, but I probably won't ever do it again."

The group went upstairs to the private rooms. "Ah, yes! The Mexican women," Nigel said. "Their presence kept things calm." He chuckled. "I thought we were going to have them sent back on that first day they arrived. That was a big brouhaha." He glanced at Rhodes. "But the regimental sergeant major got that under control."

The sound of a large vehicle was heard outside. They went out and saw a flatbed truck with a bulldozer on the trailer it was pulling. A minute later a jeep with a trailer appeared. There were three five-ton trucks. The olive drab color revealed them as the U.S. Army Engineers.

All the men got out of their vehicles and gathered around an Army Engineer major. Dwayne, Pete, Nigel, and Rhodes ambled over to see what was going on. It was a waste of time since they couldn't understand what the major was saying.

The engineer officer began, "Okay. I determined the type of material by measurement. It will take twenty-two pounds of TNT. It must be in-blown to keep the debris from flying out too far. Stack the TNT along the cement blocks. The lower we go the better."

The major and a captain walked around *The Headquarters*. Two lieutenants followed them with clipboards. When the four had gone all around three times, the lieutenants handed the officers with what they had written. The detonating cord was placed just so.

The officers went back. The enlisted men stacked the charges as the two officers watched and looked over at Dwayne and his companions. "Gentlemen! You had better go out and stand in the road."

"Wilco," Pete said.

The engineers were sure of themselves and counted down the detonating cord and firing wire. Suddenly there was a loud explosion and the pressure around the area buffeted the observers.

The Headquarters was no more.

After the dust settled, the bulldozer was backed off the flatbed trailer. The driver drove over to the rubble. A trucker came up and waited for the bulldozer operator to start scooping up and putting the rubble into the five tonners.

Dwayne, Pete, Nigel and Herbert walked over to their

car and got in. As usual Herbert drove the vehicle.

Chapter 26

It was on a Monday that F.B.I. Agent Terry McCarthy had been happy about the previous weekend. He had been playing tennis at the Prairie Wind Golf and Tennis Club with his girlfriend. This was a recreational spot that was located in Eastborough, the most affluent community of Wichita.

His fiancé's name was Lois Chapman and like McCarthy she was divorced. Lois had gone back to her parents' home after the break-up. A visit to the Prairie Wind Golf and Tennis Club and an introduction had gotten the couple together. They had been dating for six months and playing tennis was a mutual enjoyment.

After the games it was their practice to go into the club's restaurant for a couple of cocktails. When they finished, Terry and Lois went back to the Chapman mansion for a swim to cool down in the swimming pool. Afterward they didn't bother to change their clothes if the house was empty. They went upstairs to Lois' room to make love. When they finished they lounged in her bed enjoying the happy mood. After three months they decided to wed.

Lois' father was a vice president at the Boeing Airplane Company and he liked McCarthy a great deal. When Dan Chapman learned of the marriage, he approved of it. After all, her choice was an F.B.I. agent.

Now in his office, McCarthy began to feel cozy and comfortable for about five minutes until his phone rang. He frowned at the telephone then picked it up. "F.B.I."

"This is Jim Ferguson, Terry. How are you?"

"I'm enjoying life," McCarthy said. He knew Ferguson was in the U.S. Department of Justice in Washington, D.C. Those guys didn't fool around.

"You sound like you're in a good mood."

"I am," McCarthy said. "I'm going to be married. What's up?"

"Uh oh! I'm afraid I have an assignment for you."

"Well, we haven't set a date yet.

"That's good. Is that Wichita private detective Dwayne Wheeler still around?"

"I'm sure he is. We had a hell of a gunfight together in *Operation Undercover*."

"Okay, I'll get hold of him," Ferguson said. "So let me clue you in. There was an ambush of an armored truck near Shawnee, Kansas. The attack was tried by three young guys who were killed. Wheeler was driving the heavy vehicle."

"What was he doing that for?"

"It's some undercover stuff, but I don't want to discuss it now," Ferguson told him. "If I can get Wheeler to go along with you in this case, he'll be a lot of help."

"He sure will."

"Right! I'll send the documents by courier then you

can get the info from that," Ferguson said. "I'll call you back and give you Wheeler's answer."

———

THE WIDOW FORZINI AND THE OLDER SISTER Lundari were stunned by the news about Johnny and Tom. The young men were also missed by their girlfriends Sofia Vanacore and Maria Palma. Gus Augusto's death was mourned by his father who was a retired professional wrestler.

Charlie Diego, Eddie Edoardo, Rick Riccardo and Guy Maglioni were not linked to the deaths due to their retreat. When they arrived back in Boston, they were advised by oldster Carlo Tedeschi to go back to their old jobs and not discuss the botched up battle. In fact, they should lie about their absence by saying they went to Cape Cod for a short vacation.

Father Piero Bonvicini of the Immaculate Conception Church tried to raise enough money to get the three dead youngsters returned to their neighborhood cemetery in Boston. He failed because the congregation knew they had died in a criminal activity.

———

DWAYNE AND DONNA SUE HAD OPENED THEIR office early one morning. The first thing Donna Sue did was to call Millie at the Reliable Answering Service to let the young lady know they were back in action. Millie was very happy with that information.

"We've got to clean this place up, Millie" Donna Sue admitted. "It's hot and smelly so we have to air it out. But if we get any calls pass 'em on, okay?"

"You bet, Donna Sue!"

Dwayne got a bucket of water and a mop and began to swish it around the floor. He worked his part of the office and was about to start on Donna Sue's when the phone rang on her desk.

She spoke happily to Dwayne. "I think we might have some work."

Dwayne stopped mopping. "I hope so."

Donna Sue picked up the phone and said, "Dwayne Wheeler Detective Agency. Where may I send your call?"

"Hi, I'm Jim Ferguson of the Department of Justice. I would like to speak to Dwayne Wheeler."

"One moment," Donna Sue said. "Dwayne! It's the F.B.I. His name is Jim Ferguson."

Dwayne propped the mop up against the wall. "I've heard of him." He went over to the phone on his desk. "I'm Dwayne Wheeler."

"Hello, Mister Wheeler. I'm Jim Ferguson in the Department of Justice. How are you today?"

"Just fine."

"There is a special case that I would like for you to tackle. You would be working with Terry McCarthy. Are you interested?"

"I sure am. What's up?"

"I don't want to discuss it over the phone," Ferguson said. "I will be sending the material to McCarthy."

"Can I contact McCarthy now?"

"Certainly," Ferguson told him.

Dwayne hung up and turned to Donna Sue. "We might as well stop cleaning up around here. I'm going to be working with Terry McCarthy." He dialed the phone.

"McCarthy," was the brisk answer.

"Hi, McCarthy. It's me, Wheeler. I got a call from Jim Ferguson."

"What'd you tell him, Wheeler?"

"I told him yes. He told me about him mailing something or other to you."

"I'll give you a call when it shows up, then we can gallop off into the sunset."

————

The Argentine Air Force C-119 aircraft was a hundred kilometers out to sea. This was the third flight and last mission over the South Atlantic Ocean. The back of its fuselage had been removed to push the freight out into the ocean.

The cargo was body bags of Germans who had been shot in a Uruguay prison. This C-119 was operating for five of South American nations, Argentina, Bolivia, Chile, Paraguay and Uruguay.

A Nazi program was wanted after World War II by the *Waffen-SS* to create one large new Reich. This international plan was destroyed by an organization called *The Headquarters*. The building was no longer visible; not even showing itself on the Kansas prairie. There was legal tender printed new while the Germans' money failed miserably. Expert engravers saw to that.

The C-119 was pulled up slightly and the crew began to push the body bags out to fall into the South Atlantic Ocean.

CHAPTER 27

Terry McCarthy took a knife and sliced open the cardboard courier envelope. Dwayne Wheeler sat on the other side of his desk watching with great interest.

"Here we go," McCarthy said, pulling out some manila folders. "I think I'd better keep these in order." He looked at the first one. "It reads Yellow Cigarettes. What the hell are Yellow Cigarettes?" McCarthy wondered.

"They're untaxed," Dwayne said. "Those were the kind I was hauling in my truck. My *armored* truck. There were Panama City, New Orleans, Dallas, Wichita, Kansas City and Chicago on those runs. That is gone now, because of the gun fight that me and my partner had with three kids shooting submachine guns at us."

"What happened?"

"Well, it appears they didn't know we were in an armored truck," Dwayne stated. "So we opened the doors real quick and fired at the gun flashes."

"Did you and your buddy come out okay?"

"I'm here, ain't I?"

"Where's the submachine guns the bad guys had?" McCarthy inquired.

"I don't know. There was footprints back where two cars abandoned by the ambushers were. They prob'ly drove off with 'em."

"Mmm," said McCarthy. "There's nothing about a third car. Only footprints."

"I guess they didn't have a third car," Dwayne said with a shrug.

"If you say so," McCarthy said. He got another manila folder. "Okay. This one is about a couple of Treasury agents."

"Those bastards pulled a rotten trick on me. They acted like I was about two steps out of a penitentiary. They even went into our apartment and dismantled everything. I called on a Wichita lawyer by the name of Carl Banter to represent me and Donna Sue. He wrote a complaint to the Treasury Department but it didn't do any good. However, the Treasury Agents got their comeuppance when they were sent to Greenland."

"Something like that really pisses me off," McCarthy said. He read some more of the Treasury information. "For Chrissakes, Wheeler! They even blamed you for the submachine guns being gone! They were trying to cover their asses, right?"

"Yeah!"

"Here's another manila envelope," McCarthy said. He pulled it out and saw what was going to be for him and Dwayne. "Guess what? The Mafia is going to be in on this."

"I'm not surprised," Dwayne said. "We did that together once. Remember *Operation Undercover*?"

"Do I! We almost got our asses blown away," McCarthy said.

"Well, what do we start with on this *Operation Undercover*?"

"It's not really undercover," McCarthy answered. "We're supposed to go up to Shawnee, Kansas and check out those machine gunners or whatever they are, er, *were*. By the way, Wheeler, I'm going to be married. But we haven't set a date yet."

"That'll be nice, huh?"

"Well, I hope I don't get shot by some gangster before then," McCarthy said.

"You and me both."

————

TERRY MCCARTHY COLLECTED AN F.B.I. 1941 Oldsmobile for his and Dwayne's use. The first thing they did was to head for Shawnee, Kansas. They started out on U.S. 81 North and went to U.S. 50 South in Newton. From there they went through Emporia and had lunch. Next they continued on to Ottawa on U.S. 59 heading north.

They were soon back on U.S. 50 to Shawnee. They slowed down and entered the town. Dwayne had the directions to the Johnson County sheriff's office. McCarthy pulled up in front of the building and he and Dwayne went inside.

The desk sergeant looked up when the pair entered. He waited for them to identify themselves.

McCarthy wasted no time. He showed his F.B.I. identification while Dwayne showed his identification and told the desk sergeant he was working with the Feds.

"We're here to examine the three corpses of those kids."

The sergeant uttered a request. "We sure as hell hope

you came to take them away. Our morgue is cold, but not cold enough to keep those punks on an eternal spell of freshness."

"Nope," McCarthy said. "We are supposed to see if they're still here. Then to look over their possessions."

The sergeant grimaced and pressed an intercom. "Sheriff. The F.B.I. is here. They want to view those three dead kids."

The voice of the Sheriff was a happy one. "Thank the Lord! We'll get those fellows out of here."

"No, we won't," the sergeant said. "They just want to look at the bodies then check their possessions. At least I think that's what they want to do."

"Oh, Lord in Heaven! Well, send in the F.B.I."

"You heard what the Sheriff said," the sergeant uttered. "Go through that door."

Dwayne and McCarthy opened the door leading to the interior and walked down a short hall to where the Sheriff had his office. He was waiting for them while holding some keys. "Our morgue is down to the end there. Follow me."

The three men went through the door where there was a nine-drawer *corpus delicti* cabinet. The Sheriff pulled out three drawers revealing naked corpses.

Dwayne looked at their faces and wounds. "These are those Tommy gunners, alright," he said.

The Sheriff looked at him. "You were there?"

"I was there. Yeah."

McCarthy said, "The F.B.I. wants you to keep them in here until we are finished."

"What are you doing?" the Sheriff growled. He slammed the drawers shut.

"I can't tell you."

Dwayne stated, "We want to take a look at their belongings."

"Okay," the Sheriff said. "That's in the property room."

The Sheriff was followed by Dwayne and McCarthy. The possessions were in three canvas bags on a shelf. McCarthy pulled them down one at a time. He went through them very carefully. "Mmf," he said. "There's bullets holes with crusted blood around them. One of the guys defecated when the bullets hit him. The smell is pretty much gone."

"We put his underwear in a small cabinet," the Sheriff stated. "When the odor was gone, we put them with the wearer."

"Okay," McCarthy said. "We're sorry to bother you, Sheriff."

The Sheriff shrugged. "I sincerely hope we're gonna get rid of all this."

———

DWAYNE AND MCCARTHY ATE AT A RESTAURANT in Shawnee before continuing their journey. "I take it we're going to the battle site," Dwayne asked between bites of his favorite lunch, i.e. grilled cheese sandwich, French fries and Orange Crush.

"Well, tell me about the conditions we'll be traveling through," McCarthy asked. "Will it be a big adventure?"

"I know the way to the ambush and it's a rough road," Dwayne said. "I suppose it might be a little adventure."

"You and your truck driving buddy were hell on wheels, weren't you?" McCarthy said.

"If you want to get to the spot of the ambush, you won't be in comfortable driving conditions."

McCarthy chuckled. "I'll consider it an adventure."

"Well, it might be but I think we should stop at a motor court for a rest before carrying on."

"Okay, Wheeler. You take over."

Dwayne drove past Kansas City, Kansas to U.S. 40 all the way to Grain Valley. The pair stopped at a motor court and rented a cabin that was clean and close to a diner.

CHAPTER 28

The next morning Dwayne suggested that they get some food and drink in order to be comfortable while traveling through dirt rutty roads. The two travelers had a heavy breakfast each, then purchased a picnic-style meal for the afternoon snack.

They stayed on U.S. 40 for thirty minutes, then Dwayne turned off the highway and went through some small farm towns. The scenery was soon without any signs of buildings. Then they reached the road that was a track not kept very well.

Dwayne pulled to a stop. "Mess call!"

The twosome both got out and sat down on the Oldsmobile's front fenders. They opened their lunch sacks and pulled out iced tea in cardboard cups along with ham sandwiches and potato chips. As the pair ate, they gazed around their surroundings.

McCarthy took a swallow of iced tea. "I noticed you called out 'mess call.'"

"Yep," Dwayne said chewing on his sandwich. "I was in the Army. Even before the war started."

"Y'know," McCarthy said, "of all the time we've spent together we never discussed our military experience."

"Well, I was a military policeman who played in the black market. I got caught and was given a discharge for the Convenience of the Government. I'm a private detective because I couldn't get a job on the Wichita Police Department or the Kansas Highway Patrol or the Kansas Bureau of Investigation or the Federal Bureau of Investigation."

"Did you try all those outfits, Dwayne?"

"You should know. Tell me about your career."

"I was in Harvard University when Pearl Harbor was bombed. I hurried to the nearest recruiting station to join the Army."

"I bet you went to Officers Candidate School. Right?"

"Right," McCarthy said. "I ended up with an artillery commission and was wounded in the D-Day operation. That was on the third day and I was sent back to England to a hospital. They patched me up pretty good and I was returned to my unit."

Both ate in silence for the next twenty minutes.

"Okay," Dwayne said. "Let's go."

They threw their trash bags down and got into the Oldsmobile.

———

THE TRACK GREW ROUGHER THE FARTHER THEY traveled. The armored truck was heavy enough to simply roll a bit, but the Oldsmobile was bouncing up and down.

There was a rise in the distance, and Dwayne headed for it. When he got over the small hill, he stopped and pointed. "There's the cars."

Dwayne drove down and then up to the cars. They

got out and walked over to the vehicles. McCarthy looked inside each. "Nobody was killed in the interior of these automobiles."

"Nope," Dwayne said. He pointed to the ground. "There were some footprints here but I guess the winds and rains have blown them away."

McCarthy looked at Dwayne. "I guess that's about all, right?"

"Yep."

"Okay. I'll drive for a while."

———

THE JOURNEY TOOK TWO DAYS IN WHICH McCarthy drove all the way. The F.B.I. safehouse was located in the Jefferson Ward of Boston. McCarthy turned into a driveway that circled around to the back of a one-story frame dwelling.

McCarthy came to a stop and he and Dwayne got out of the Oldsmobile. The two yawned and stretched. Dwayne drew a Lucky Strike out of his cigarette pack. "I appreciate you doing all that driving."

"Well, you had the wheel over the tough terrain."

The back door opened and a swarthy, muscular man stepped out to walk across a small porch. "Don't tell me," he said with a laugh. "You must be Wheeler and McCarthy."

"That's us," McCarthy said.

The man held his hand out. "I'm Sam Sica. Actually Salvatore Sica. But call me Sam, okay?" He walked over to a multi-garage and opened the last door. "You can park that Oldsmobile in there. We don't want a Kansas car discovered around here in the Jefferson Ward."

McCarthy drove the car into the garage.

"Get your luggage and I'll take you to your bedrooms."

Sam led them across the porch and into the house. He took them down a narrow hall. "You guys choose which bedroom you want. One is as good as the other so settle in. You're lucky because all the bedrooms are empty. There are closets."

"What about shaving, etcetera?" McCarthy asked.

"Each of these have a sink with a mirror. There are two bathrooms and two showers down the hall. There is a large refrigerator holding various drinks and ice."

"That's fine," Dwayne said.

Sam left them and Dwayne and McCarthy simply walked in the bedrooms closest to each of them. The bedcovers were not made yet, so they took care of that. Their next brief chore was to open their luggage. The clothes went into the closet while their toilette was put on a small desk.

"God damn it!" McCarthy said. "I'm gonna write a letter to J. Edgar Hoover about this! Wichita has a much better safehouse with a kitchen and cook."

"Sign my name on any complaint," Dwayne said. "In the meantime I'm gonna take a nap."

———

DWAYNE AND MCCARTHY WOKE UP ABOUT THE same time. But it was McCarthy who was up first and he walked over to Dwayne's bedroom. He could hear the water running as Dwayne was shaving.

"Hey, Wheeler!"

"Yeah?"

"I think we're gonna have to leave this safehouse to get something to eat."

"Alright," Dwayne said. "I'm almost finished shaving."

McCarthy opened the door and entered. "I can't find that Sam Sica anywhere."

Dwayne wiped the shaving soap off his face. "Right now I don't give a shit about that landlord or whatever he is."

"He's an F.B.I. agent, of course."

Dwayne put on his watch showing eight o'clock p.m. "Let's go hunt up a restaurant."

They were both dressed nonchalantly in a blue cotton shirt for Dwayne; checkered red and black flannel for McCarthy; and both were wearing khaki pants. They also had brown shoes and brown fedoras. The two walked around the safehouse and down an alley.

The pair walked two blocks and sighted a small commercial market area and sauntered into it. "Ah!" McCarthy said. "There's a restaurant with a welcoming sign. See? *The Pancake and Waffle Café*."

The two went inside and sat down. They ordered a coffee each from the waitress. She came back with two mugs and asked, "Whatta ya want? Pancakes or waffles?"

"Pancakes," Dwayne and McCarthy declared in unison a second time.

"Big or little?"

"Big," Dwayne and McCarthy declared in unison once again.

The service was quick and Dwayne and McCarthy asked for another mug of coffee each. When that was finished, they left a rather large tip for the waitress. When they walked out of the restaurant she said a sincere, "My name is Rose. Come back the next time you two are hungry."

_____

When Dwayne and McCarthy got back to the safehouse it was still empty. Dwayne decided to take a nap in his bedroom while McCarthy began writing a letter to his fiancé Lois Chapman.

An hour later Sam Sica showed up with a Boston police Lieutenant by the name of Gerald Harrigan. He was a big man with a rugged face and Sica put the Irishman in his small office. Sica butted in on Dwayne's nap along with McCarthy's letter writing.

"Okay! Your policeman is this way."

He led the two down to his office and opened the door, sticking his nose in. "Lieutenant Harrigan here will give you any information you need."

Harrigan looked at McCarthy and chuckled. "Now there's an Irishman if ever I saw one." He switched his eyes to Dwayne. "And here's a brave man for sure. So now allow me to shake both your hands. What sort of information do you need?"

McCarthy pulled his notebook out of his pocket. "The main thing we have to do is find out if there is or is not a Mafia family here in the Jefferson Ward."

"There is none," Harrigan said. "At one time there was two families. That was the Forzinis and Lundaris. But they were wiped out when they wanted to establish something or another in the Midwest."

Dwayne lit a cigarette. "Is there a chance that those Mafia families have come back?"

"Not to our knowledge," Harrigan said. "The closest to that was the death of three young guys." He pulled his notebook out. "Yeah. There was Johnny Forzini, Tom Lundari and Gus Augusto. Forzini and Lundari were punks who were playing Mafia to do something their dads did. The other guy was Augusto who was a muscle champion or something. Anyhow, they all got killed trying to rob somebody. We don't know who."

"We know all about that," Dwayne said. "Their bodies are still in a police morgue in Shawnee, Kansas."

"The Boston police don't know anything about that," Harrigan said. "If you guys want, go to the Forzini and Lundari family homes." He scribbled in his notebook and tore off a page. "Here's their addresses."

"Okay," McCarthy said, standing up. "Thanks for the information."

"It wasn't much," Harrigan said. "But I can do some looking around. If I find something, I'll let you know."

Dwayne and McCarthy watched him leave. "You know something, McCarthy? We're gonna be butting heads."

CHAPTER 29

D wayne and McCarthy left their Oldsmobile with their out of town Kansas license plates in the garage. The pair got a '35 DeSoto Airflow Business Coupé. They got out their suits to be cleaned at a neighborhood cleaners that Sam Sica told them about. With that done the pair shined their shoes and got their briefcases.

Their first task that afternoon was to visit the Forzini home. A knock on the door brought a middle-aged woman in a faded dress. Terry McCarthy spoke politely showing his I.D. card as did Dwayne.

"Good afternoon, ma'am. We are agents of the F.B.I. and would like to speak with you."

She was hesitant and didn't open the screen door. "What is it you want?"

"Are you Mrs. Forzini?"

"I am *Miss* Blanche Forzini, his daughter. What do you want?"

Dwayne spoke courteously. "It is about Johnny Forzini, ma'am."

"Oh my God!" she said, turning and calling out. "Ma! Ma! Oh, God!"

An elderly woman appeared also not well dressed. "What is happening!"

"A man is here talking about Johnny!"

She glanced at Dwayne and McCarthy. "What have you done with Johnny? We know he is in Kansas and dead." The old lady began weeping. The daughter turned and helped her over to the sofa.

She turned to Dwayne and McCarthy. "You can come in."

The two men let themselves into the living room. "Thank you," Dwayne said.

"We'll try to be quick," McCarthy assured her.

Mrs. Forzini sat silently then spoke. "I knew this was going to happen. Joe was evil. He should have taken better care of Johnny."

"Who was Joe?" Dwayne asked.

Blanche said, "He was our father who was a Mafia boss. But he was killed and the whole organization was wiped out in the Midwest somewhere."

Dwayne and McCarthy knew that would have been in the *Undercover Operation*.

Blanche cleared her throat. "Can we get Johnny's body to bury now?"

"We don't have that information but you can try," McCarthy said. "You would have to write to the Johnson County Sheriff in Shawnee, Kansas."

"Wait a moment, please," Blanche said. She got up and walked over to a small table. She opened a drawer and pulled out paper and pencil. "What was that address again?"

"Johnson County Sheriff, Shawnee, Kansas," McCarthy said. He knew she probably wouldn't get her brother's body for a long time if ever. She wrote it down and looked up at her mother. "Can you answer some questions for us, Miss Forzini?"

"Yes. Of course."

"I'm sure you have been questioned before," McCarthy said. "But I hope you'll understand that we have to do this." He cleared his throat. "Was Johnny connected to any gang?"

"I'm not sure," Blanche said. "He quit his job."

Mrs. Forzini cried. "His papa was evil! He left Johnny guns and money!" She calmed down and looked at the visitors. "There's thousands of dollars up in his room. He didn't spend it all. Dollars that are evil. Dollars that belong to Satan."

Blanche was angry and frightened by what her mother said. "She doesn't know what she's saying! There's no money up in his room!"

"Yes there is!" Mrs. Forzini said. "Shut up!"

"No, Ma," Blanche said. "If there's any money up there I'll go see. And if there is I'll tell Father Piero about it. He'll know what to do."

Dwayne and McCarthy knew they would get no information from the Forzini family. "Well," Dwayne said. "Did Johnny have any friends?"

"His friends are laying up in Kansas like him," Blanche said. "He had a girlfriend here in the Ward."

"How about a name and address?" Dwayne asked.

Blanche walked back over to the table and wrote down the requested information. "Here."

"We'll be going now. Thank you for talking with us."

"Yes," McCarthy said. He closed his briefcase and the two men left the house.

Dwayne said, "Well, if there's thousands of dollars

then the daughter will either take it to a priest or go hide it someplace else."

"I'll bet she's spent the money," McCarthy opined.

Dwayne pointed. "There's the Lundari's house."

"Let's just request info about gangs, okay?" McCarthy said.

The visit to the Lundaris was nothing but trying to get Tom Lundari's corpse home. They got the name and address of his girlfriend, too.

When they visited Gus Augusto's dad the old wrestler got upset. "My boy is dead. I don't want to talk about it. Go away. If you don't, I'll come out there and break your necks."

Dwayne and McCarthy decided that retreating was prudent.

The next thing Dwayne and McCarthy did was to visit the girlfriends. Sofia Vanacore was the first. When her mother heard the knock on the door, she was instantly alarmed. "What do you want?"

"We would like to speak to your daughter," Dwayne said. "It's about her boyfriend."

She slammed the door.

They walked toward the Palma house. "Mmm," McCarthy said. "I bet we'll get the same treatment where the other girl lives."

When they knocked on the door, a teenage girl answered. "Yes?" she said.

"We would like to speak to Maria Palma," McCarthy said.

"I'm Maria."

"We would like to speak to you about Tom Lundari."

The girl burst out crying.

A woman came running. "What's the trouble?"

Maria wiped her eyes. "They want to know about Tommy."

Dwayne quickly spoke as he showed his I.D. card. "We're in the Federal Bureau of Investigation, ma'am. We would like to get some information about Tom Lundari."

Mrs. Palma was politer than the Forzini women. "Maria was dating him regularly, then he was killed. He's buried in Kansas, I think."

"His body is in Kansas but not buried," McCarthy said.

"I don't understand," Mrs. Palma said.

"He is in a corpus delicti drawer," Dwayne said.

She grew angry. "I have no idea what you're talking about."

"Well," Dwayne said. "It's a cabinet for dead people."

She slammed the door.

Dwayne and McCarthy walked off the porch and turned back toward the shopping center. They had grown bored trying to find things indicating that the Mafia had returned to this neighborhood.

CHAPTER 30

E dgar Kummel owned a beer tavern in the Industrial District of the Jefferson Ward. Every working day Edgar, a husky German-American, came in at 5:30 a.m. to get the coffee, beer and whiskey shots ready for the laborers before they went to work.

There were no unions in the district so the workers labored 12 hours a day, meaning a 72-hour week. Edgar was a cheerful man who was popular with his customers. As long as one laborer could stand up, Edgar would remain behind his bar until the drunk staggered out.

The dawn sun was just above the horizon when Edgar pulled up in his '35 Ford behind his tavern. He went into the back room, switched on the lights and began getting bottles of beer to take out to the drinking area. He worked for a half hour to get the lot under the counter. Then he turned to fill the large coffee pot and turned it on. With all that done he walked up to the front door and unlocked it.

Three of his best customers showed up on time and walked in. These were three welders who worked in a machine shop close by. Edgar set three bottles of beer up on the bar then reached down and pulled up three shot glasses. He poured whiskey in those and stepped back.

Edgar laughed. "Is that gonna get you ready for the day's work?"

"You got it!" one of the welders said.

Now other customers, laborers and skilled workers, came in for beer, shots and coffee. As more men came in the louder it got with laughs or growls about the good and bad foremen.

After a half-hour the noise stopped as the customers left the tavern. Edgar cleared out the empty bottles and turned to wash the glassware in the sink behind the bar. The bell over the door rang and a man in a business suit stepped in.

"Hi ya, Kummel. How's things? It's me, the Insurance Man."

Edgar didn't like the caller. He didn't answer but walked over to the cash register and pulled out fifteen dollars. He handed three five-dollar bills over to the suave man.

"Until next week, Kummel."

———

DWAYNE WHEELER AND TERRY MCCARTHY decided to call on the local church. They figured a priest might be friendly to the F.B.I. After eating at the *Pancake and Waffles Café* they asked Rose the waitress where the nearest church was located.

"It's three streets over that way," Rose said, laughing and pointing. "Are you two gonna confess your sins?"

"Probably," McCarthy said with a grin. "Is it a Catholic church?"

"It's the only Catholic Church in Jefferson Ward," Rose said. "In fact it's the only church in the Ward."

McCarthy laughed out loud. "Then Dwayne won't get a blessing. He's a Protestant."

"Actually I ain't got any religion," Dwayne said.

They walked the three blocks and came to the church and went up the steps to the door. Dwayne pulled them open and gestured for McCarthy to enter ahead of him. The interior of the church was semi-dark and McCarthy headed toward the altar.

"Where are we going?"

"The presbytery."

"What's the presbytery?" Dwayne asked.

"It's the priest's office," McCarthy said as he approached it. He knocked on the door.

A voice in the interior spoke. "Come in."

McCarthy led the way. "Good morning, Father."

Dwayne decided to stay silent.

The priest seated behind his desk was friendly. "Good morning. What can I do for you gentlemen?"

McCarthy pulled out his identification and showed it to him. "F.B.I."

Dwayne sucked in a breath and spoke, "F.B.I."

"I am Father Piero Bonvicini."

"We're here to see about crime in the Ward," McCarthy explained. "Particularly the Mafia."

The priest said, "We haven't had the Mafia here for two or three years."

McCarthy pulled out his notebook. "I have some names. John Forzini, Tom Lundari and Gus Augusto. Are you familiar with their names?"

"Of course," Father Piero said. "But if you're looking for those boys, you are too late. They are dead."

"We know that, Father," McCarthy said. "In fact, we saw their corpses in Shawnee, Kansas a week or so ago."

Father Piero was sentimental. "I've tried to get the congregation to bring them back here, but they won't pay to get those lads returned. Most of the worshipers curse them for being criminals. And their families don't have enough money to get their sons' bodies."

Dwayne looked at McCarthy. "I think we're done with our assignment. So it's back to Wichita."

"Wait!" Father Piero stated. "There is something else besides the Mafia."

"What would that be?" McCarthy asked.

"I cannot violate the sanctity of the confessional," the priest said, "but if you go to the Ristorante Italiana and ask for Carlo Tedeschi the owner, you might be able to take care of another type of crime."

"What is that foreign language?" Dwayne asked.

"It means 'Italian Restaurant'."

"Where is this Italian Restaurant?" Dwayne inquired.

"Go two blocks north and one east."

"Thank you, Father," McCarthy said.

"Go with God, my son."

They left the office and the church.

"Whataya think?" Dwayne asked as they walked along. "It's kind of late."

"You're right, Wheeler. Let's go back to the safehouse and discuss this."

They left the small area and stopped at a take-away restaurant named Hamburgers Incorporated. Along with the hamburgers were French fries and chocolate milkshakes. When Dwayne and McCarthy returned to the safehouse they found Sam Sica sitting in the back yard.

"Hey, guys. Lieutenant Harrigan was here looking for you."

"What do you mean 'looking' for us?" Dwayne asked.

Sica shrugged. "What do I know? You got something to hide?"

Dwayne said, "Just for that sarcasm, we aren't gonna share these French fries with you."

CHAPTER 31

D wayne and McCarthy were seated at a table with a sun umbrella in the backyard of the safehouse the next early afternoon. They were waiting for Lieutenant Harrigan to come for a visit to discuss what had been going on.

McCarthy stretched and lit a cigarette. "You know something, Wheeler, I've been thinking."

Dwayne chuckled. "Really? You don't do that very much."

"Ha! Ha! You're so funny. But my thoughts have been about us addressing each other by our surnames."

Dwayne thought a moment. "That's true, McCarthy." He lit a Lucky Strike. "I supposed it's just a habit, hey?"

"We've been through a lot together. There's the *Operation Undercover* with the Mafia where we had to fight ourselves out on that hellish night. And now this caper as you private detectives say. I think we should call each other by our first names."

"Sure," Dwayne said. "Terry."

"Okay then, Dwayne."

They were interrupted by a police car coming into the yard and parking in front of the garages. Lieutenant Harrigan got out. "Hello, guys." He walked over and joined them under the sun umbrella.

"How're you doing?" Terry asked.

"Let's say it's how you're doing?" Harrigan countered.

"Well," Dwayne said. "We're pretty sure that the Jefferson Ward has no Mafia."

The policeman said, "I could have told you that. So! Is there going to be a wrap up?"

"Yeah," Terry said. He and Dwayne did not want him to know a thing about their operation. "We're gonna look around some more."

"Well," Harrigan said, standing up. "Have fun."

Dwayne and Terry gave Lieutenant Harrigan time to leave, then the pair got into the DeSoto Airflow Coupe. Terry drove over to the Ristorante Italiana and parked down the street.

Dwayne and Terry walked up to the front door of the restaurant. They tried the door and found it locked. Dwayne knocked hard. A voice came from inside. "We're not open."

"We're F.B.I."

The curtain over the door glass was pulled to one side. It was old Carlo Tedeschi. He opened the door. "Come in."

Dwayne and Terry entered and were impressed by the interior. They showed their credentials and Tedeschi gave them a careful look. "My name is Carlo Tedeschi. I'm the owner of this restaurant."

Terry said, "I'm Agent McCarthy and this is Agent Wheeler."

"What can I do for you, gentlemen?"

"We need some information that Father Bonvicini said you could give us," Terry said.

"Oh!" Tedeschi said. "Let's go to my office."

Dwayne and Terry followed him to a door that opened into a small room with a desk and chairs. They all sat down and Terry started the conversation. "We visited the priest to see about the dead youngsters in Kansas. He said he was trying to get them back home."

"Yes," Tedeschi said. "And it's a shame."

"There's another item," Terry said.

"What is that?" Tedeschi inquired.

"He said there was no Mafia here," Terry said.

"The priest was right," Tedeschi said. "But it wasn't so long ago that we had two Mafia groups here. But they were wiped out in some crazy stuff in Kansas."

"Then he said we should go and see you about another problem. We'd like to find out about it."

Tedeschi gritted his teeth. "I wish he hadn't done that."

"Why?" Dwayne asked.

Tedeschi was frightened and didn't say anything.

Terry was curious. "Is there somebody that will kill you if you give us any information?"

Tedeschi didn't say anything, but he was obviously wanting to reveal something dangerous.

Dwayne studied him. "What if we give you three days to think this over? I can see you're nervous as hell but want to reveal something."

The old man's hands were trembling. "Yes. Yes. Let's do that."

———

KAY CHAUCET WAS ARRANGING SEVERAL flowers for a wedding when the bell over the door jangled. She walked out to her reception area and saw the person who had come in.

"Hello, Sweetheart," he said. "It is me, the Insurance Man."

Kay got an envelope she had put fifteen dollars in and handed it over.

"Until next week, Miss Bouquets."

———

DWAYNE WAS SITTING ON HIS BED WHILE TERRY was occupying his chair. They were both drinking Coca-Cola. "What's your call on that old Tedeschi?" Dwayne asked Terry.

"My call? He's scared shitless!"

"Listen to me then," Dwayne said. "During the old Mafia days back in Prohibition, every day was rough for the poverty-stricken population. But Mafia dons treated them right. They even sent doctors to poor people who had sick kids. The residents did the Mafia favors like hiding secret things in their apartments, making hooch for them in their bathtubs and all that kind of stuff."

"Yeah. I got that in F.B.I. training."

"So Tedeschi is scared about something, right?"

"Right," Terry said.

"What we're gonna have to do is figure out if Tedeschi is a lone scared old man or he's part of a large crowd. A crowd the size of the Jefferson Ward."

"You know what we gotta do," Terry opined. "Let's go to the police sub-station here and see what Lieutenant Harrigan thinks."

"Sure, Terry. We got three days."

———

DWAYNE WHEELER AND TERRY MCCARTHY GOT out of the DeSoto and walked into the Jefferson Ward Police Sub-Station and up to the desk sergeant. "Is Harrigan in?"

"What's it to you?" the sergeant grumbled.

"We're F.B.I. and staying in the F.B.I," Terry said. "So tell us, is Lieutenant Harrigan in? Here's our credentials. Show yours, Dwayne."

"Why didn't you say so," the sergeant said. He pushed the intercom. "Lieutenant, there's some F.B.I.s out here to see you."

"Send 'em in," Harrigan said.

"Straight back through that door," the sergeant said.

Dwayne and Terry entered a hallway and walked to the office with Harrigan's name on the door. They entered without knocking.

The Lieutenant stood up and offered his hand. "What's up, guys? It must be something important."

"Yep," Terry said. "We went to the Ristorante Italiana and met with Carlo Tedeschi."

"Uh. Oh," Harrigan said with a grin.

"He's worried as hell about something," Dwayne said.

Harrigan laughed. "That's old Carlo, guys. He's as crazy as can be."

"Really?" Terry said.

"Yeah," Harrigan said. "He calls here two or three times every month about some crazy nothing. We coddle him. Don't give him any attention."

"Okay," Dwayne said. He turned to Terry. "We can forget that right now and turn to something else."

"Right," Terry said.

They left the police sub-station and got into the

DeSoto. Dwayne was driving. "You know something, Terry?"

"Hell, yes! That Harrigan was lying to us."

————

BERT DELIANA, OWNER OF *HAMBURGERS Incorporated*, took twenty dollars out of his cash register. He handed it over to the Insurance Man.

"Until next week, DeLiana."

CHAPTER 32

Since they had three days before going back to Carlo Tedeschi, Dwayne and Terry sat under the tree behind the safehouse. They had some bottles of beer in a bucketful of ice that they were enjoying.

The pair didn't talk much, they just drank the beer and belched. Sam Sica drove the Government Buick around in the safehouse and parked it in the nearest garage. He got out and walked rapidly up to Dwayne and Terry with a fierce frown on his face.

"I gotta talk to you two, God damn it!"

Terry frowned. "What's your problem?"

Sam helped himself to one of the beers and opened it. "I hear you visited Carlo Tedeschi."

"Yeah," Dwayne growled irritably. "Who told you?"

"At this point in the operation I'm not gonna tell you," Sam stated.

"What operation?" Terry asked him.

"My operation, God damn it!"

"Whoa!" Dwayne said.

"Did you go to Lieutenant Harrigan?" Sam asked.

"Yeah," Dwayne said now upset.

Sam started to yell but stopped and was silent for a full five seconds. "Okay! I'm gonna get you guys into it."

"Into what?" Dwayne asked.

"Into the operation," Sam stated. "Tell me, what did you think of the Lieutenant?"

Terry spoke out. "He's a bad guy."

Sam got another beer. "Did you let him know what you thought of him?"

"No we did not," Dwayne told him.

Sam took a drink. "I'm glad you were smart enough to recognize that. Because if he knew we were on to him, the operation would have collapsed. You see, guys, I have been on to him, too. And there's the weekly payoffs that have been going in Jefferson Ward. Somebody's shaking down the businesses. We don't know his name except that he calls himself the Insurance Man."

"Wow!" Dwayne exclaimed. "You're way ahead of us, Sam."

Terry was curious. "Why don't we just sneak up on him when he gets a payoff and arrest him."

"For three reasons," Sam said. "If we did that he would get jailed. Then we wouldn't be able to know who he's working for and how many there are of others doing the same thing."

"Maybe he *is* a Mafioso," Terry contributed.

"You may be right but I doubt it," Sam said. "I don't know how many Insurance Men there are. We've got to dig up a lot of things on that gang."

Dwayne shrugged. "Now we're going to go after a hidden crime group just like we're supposed to."

Sam smiled. "Y'know something. I really like you two guys!"

Maurizio Luna was a shoemaker who had been in the U.S.A. since 1925. He was repairing an expensive oxford shoe when he heard his name called.

"Hello, Maurizio," the voice said. "It is me, the Insurance Man."

Maurizio stopped his work and went over to a cigar box on his counter. He pulled out a five dollar bill and gave it to the caller.

"Until next week, Mister Luna."

When the three days they had given Carlo Tedeschi were up, the F.B.I. agents visited the elderly man. Dwayne was the driver of the Buick, Sam Sica was the leading agent, and Terry was the passenger.

It was agreed among the F.B.I. agents that Carlo would get into Sam's car after dark. Terry walked up to his house and knocked on the door. Carlo showed up and indicated he would go with him.

"I thought over the three days and I'm ready to go with you fellers. I'm paying insurance, too."

The two went to the Buick and Carlo got into the back seat. "He's gonna work with us," Terry said.

"Okay, Carlo," Sam said as Dwayne put the car into gear. "We need you."

"What do I do, Sam?" Carlo asked.

"Is there any guys you know who are paying the Insurance Man? They gotta be gutsy. Know what I mean?"

"Sure," Carlo said. "Let me think. Mmm. I'll ask Edgar Kummel. He's got a tavern and he's tough as nails.

But he knows there are people scared to death. So he's paying the Insurance Man."

"The four of us could visit Edgar Kummel when the Insurance Man shows up to be paid," Dwayne suggested.

"Where would we take him?" Sam said.

"If you want to take two subjects at once," Terry said, "it would be the Jefferson Ward Police Sub-Station and arrest Lieutenant Harrigan at the same time we got the Insurance Man."

Old Carlo was enthusiastic. "I could call Edgar and find out what days he has to pay up."

"Okay. I'll take you back home," Sam said. He reached in his inside jacket pocket and pulled out a card. "This has my phone number."

After they left Carlo, the agents went back to the safe-house. They put the car away and went inside to sit around the outdoor table drinking Coke. Sam said, "I got to call Jim Ferguson."

"Oh, yeah," Terry said. "He's the guy in Washington that got ahold of me. He also knows about Dwayne."

"That's Jim Ferguson for you," Sam said. "I better call him at home since its night."

He dialed the operator and asked for long distance. He hung up and waited for the call to be completed.

Dwayne had been to the liquor store earlier in the day. He went to his bedroom. He had purchased a couple of fifths of Jack Daniels Sour Mash Whiskey. He got the bottle out and poured the glasses.

Sam took a sip. "Hey! This is what I call liquor!"

"Agreed!" Terry said. "Dwayne gave me some while we were on *Operation Undercover*. Smooth, huh?"

"Well," Dwayne said. "Let's figure out a name for this operation."

"Good idea," Sam said. "How about Operation Jack Daniels Sour Mash?"

"Too long," Terry said.

"You're absolutely right, Terry," Dwayne agreed. He looked at their empty glasses. "Anybody want another snort?"

Everyone's glasses were refilled and the phone rang. Sam answered it. "Is that you, Jim? Yeah. Everything is going well. Yeah. There's a merchant here that's gonna help us. We're gonna pick up the Insurance Man. No. We don't know if it's a real Insurance Man. No, we don't know his real name. Dwayne Wheeler and Terry McCarthy are here and agree that Harrigan is crooked as a dog's hind legs. You want us to arrest Lieutenant Harrigan then? Well, we've had some suspicions of him but weren't quite sure. Okay then. We'll put him in jail with the Insurance Man as soon as we arrest him. Okay, Jim. So you're going to fly up here tomorrow? Out."

Sam hung up. "Now things are really going to be jumping around here." He looked at Dwayne. "Where's that Jack Daniels? I'm a thirsty man!"

———

ALEX BRUKARZ WAS THE OWNER OF A SMALL print shop. He was working on his Linotype when he heard the bell ringing out by his counter. He knew who it was and picked up an envelope containing twenty-five dollars. He went to the counter.

"It's me the, Insurance Man."

Alex gave him the money.

"Until next week, Mister Brukarz."

———

THE F.B.I. GUYS DRANK CUPS OF COFFEE AND were impatient for Jim Ferguson to show up from Washington.

Dwayne was the only man not to know Ferguson. "What's he like?"

Terry answered, "Don't worry. You'll find out."

Sam shrugged. "There's a lot of people who are useful in this merry game we play who don't know their value."

Dwayne raised his cup and declared, "Here's to heroes who are unknown, secret, obscure and mysterious."

"Here! Here!" Terry and Sam said in unison.

CHAPTER 33

Edgar Kummel was going to spring a surprise on the Insurance Man. He was in his tavern while Dwayne Wheeler, Terry McCarthy and Sam Sica were in the back. This latter three were armed with automatic pistols.

The working men who had come in for beer before going to work had been gone for fifteen minutes and the tavern was empty. The F.B.I. men smoked and turned down Edgar's offers of beer. However, they took cups of coffee from the urn up front.

It was about a half an hour passed when the sound of the front door opening and closing was heard in the back. The F.B.I. agents were ready. They knew Edgar was behind the counter.

"Hi ya, Kummel. I'm the Insurance Man."

Edgar said, "I know who you are."

Edgar could be heard in the back of the tavern walking over to the cash register. He rang up the cash register a number of times. That was the signal for the F.B.I. group to spring into action.

The bell went off and they went around the counter.

The Insurance Man tried to get away, but Dwayne grabbed him and dragged him back.

"No you don't, asshole!" he said.

The Insurance Man was angry. "You bastards are making a big mistake!"

Handcuffs were put on the Insurance Man and they dragged him out of the rear door. The prisoner was thrown into the back of the Buick by Dwayne and Terry. They got on both sides of him while Sam started the car.

"Here we come!" Sam sang out. "We're gonna dance into the Jefferson Ward Police Sub-Station."

Ten minutes later the F.B.I. pulled up in front of the destination. Dwayne pulled the Insurance Man out of the rear door. Terry trotted around to get on the other side. Sam joined them and they went through the sub-station's door.

The desk sergeant Lee Bascom jumped up. "What do we have here?"

"A prisoner," Sam said.

"I can see it's a prisoner," the sergeant said. "But what's he charged for?"

Sam looked into the sergeant's face. "You're gonna play an important part in this activity!"

"Uh, okay."

Lieutenant Gerald Harrigan heard the noise and came out of his office. He saw the Insurance Man and looked badly surprised. "Take that guy back to the cells," he said nervously.

Dwayne walked over to Lieutenant Harrigan and pulled his revolver out of his holster. Harrigan looked at him confused. "What the hell are you doing?"

Sam took the revolver from Dwayne. "Gerald Harrigan, you are under Federal arrest. I've been ordered to do that by F.B.I. agent Jim Ferguson."

"You go to hell," Harrigan protested. "I don't even know him."

"Well, he knows you," Sam said. "So it's to the jail-house you go."

Harrigan got nasty and grabbed his revolver from Sam, but Dwayne was quick and knocked the weapon out of his hand.

Terry twirled Harrigan around and quickly put hand-cuffs on him. The next arrest was Sergeant Lee Bascom. Dwayne took his pistol and cuffed him. "Okay. Bascom, you are also under Federal arrest."

Sam Sica led the way to the entry room that had a camera and fingerprinting paraphernalia. They took the three prisoners in and had a hell of a time getting Harrigan to go through the entrance routine. He finally gave up his badge and holster but not willingly. After getting his picture taken and fingerprinted, Harrigan gave in.

Bascom gave no resistance to stand for the camera and have his fingerprinting done. When it was the Insurance Man's turn he emptied his pockets and Sam saw a driver's license.

"Ah, here's your name," Sam remarked. He looked at Dwayne and Terry. "Gentlemen, meet Bradford Jameson."

There were already three prisoners in the six lockups and they were surprised to see who was going to join them. The lawmen put Harrigan in the front cell, Jameson in the third cell and Bascom the fifth in the rear.

"Why are those three guys already in here?" Dwayne pondered.

Terry looked them up. "Drunk driving, behind ex-wife's child's payment and, last but not least, a guy driving without a driver's license."

"Well, this is an F.B.I. operation," Sam said. "So you, Dwayne and Terry, call to the Boston Police Headquarters to send a paddy wagon to take them downtown." He looked at his watch. "Okay, I've got to drive to Bradly Government Field north of the city to get Jim Ferguson and a couple of other guys. So you hang around to get those three other prisoners transferred."

"Okay, you guys," Dwayne said. "You're gonna be moving out of here and into the Central Jail."

———

ROSE OF THE *PANCAKE AND WAFFLE CAFÉ* WENT to the window in the kitchen wall and turned in the customer's order. The owner, Ronald DeLiana, came out and walked to the door. He looked in two directions then came back.

Rose said, "Don't worry about it."

Ronald took a deep breath then exhaled. "I don't know. The Insurance Man is a sneaky bastard."

"It's not your fault if he's late," Rose said.

"Yeah," Ronald said. "You're probably right."

———

DWAYNE AND TERRY HAD TURNED THE THREE original prisoners over to the cops from the central station.

The Buick showed up at the curb. Sam had picked up Jim Ferguson, George Duncan and Boris Leavenway. They got out and all four went into the sub-station. Sam introduced them to Dwayne.

Jim Ferguson shook his hand. "I was glad to hear you were going to be with us, Wheeler. Terry McCarthy had sent your name to the F.B.I. as being one hell of a good man. He said you two guys were hell on wheels in the *Undercover Operation.*"

"Thanks," Dwayne said.

"And I'll introduce you to George Duncan and Boris Leavenway."

"Glad to know you guys," Dwayne said.

Terry smiled at Duncan and Leavenway. "I know you guys!"

"Let's go into the cells," Sam said. "There's three prisoners. Lee Bascom is in the first cell, Bradford Jameson in the center and Gerald Harrigan is down in the last cell."

Jim Ferguson walked down to the end of the cells. He saw Harrigan sleeping on a bunk. "Hey! Wake up!"

Harrigan opened his eyes and looked at Ferguson. "What the hell do you want?" he growled.

"I want to see what a crooked cop looks like," Ferguson said.

Harrigan got up and walked to the bars. "D'you know I can give you a lot of information?"

"I might look into that," Ferguson said. "But I think I can do better with Sergeant Bascom up at the front of the jail. Or that other guy Jameson."

He went to the middle cell where Bradford Jameson was looking out the barred window. He turned around.

"Hey, bud," Ferguson said, walking up to the bars.

"Is there any way I can get a break?"

"What's your part in all this?"

"I'm the Insurance Man, Bradford Jameson. I worked with Harrigan and Bascom. We set up a phony deal where the local merchants were told they had to have some insurance or close up. Harrigan made it look like it was on the up-and-up."

"Well, that's real interesting," Ferguson said. "How much money were you pulling in?"

"Two hundred bucks a week," Jameson replied. "Harrigan got one hundred bucks, Bascom got twenty-five bucks and I got seventy-five bucks."

"How long did that last?" Ferguson asked.

"Well, let's see," he said. "It started forty months ago so we pulled in a total of four thousand bucks. So it's all over now."

"What's your status with all this money?"

"Well, Harrigan and I are uncle and nephew," Jameson said. "Bascom is an old friend of Harrigan's."

"Do you have a bank account?"

"Nope. I squandered my cash in one of those floating card games that are always playing around the city." He got a hopeful look in his eyes. "Can I get a break if I tell who runs those games?"

"We're F.B.I.," Jameson said, "and don't work that sort of thing."

CHAPTER 34

It took Dwayne and Terry three days to travel in the '41 Oldsmobile from Boston to Wichita. After arriving at the Jax Downtown Parking, Dwayne turned the auto in and put it in a stall. The two had called their wives from the town of Newton saying they wanted them to pick them up by the curbs.

Husbands and wives kissed and embraced, then Dwayne and Donna Sue got in the Nash Station Wagon and headed for home. Terry McCarthy and Lois Chapman went to their Cadillac and drove to her home in Eastborough. Luckily for them her father and mother were on vacation.

Dwayne was on the way to the EZ Parking Garage. "Anything new?"

"Yes," Donna Sue said. "I was to call you for Benny Gordon. It's about Western Danceland."

"Well, he's gotta wait until tomorrow," Dwayne said.

Donna Sue shifted in the seat and placed her hand on his leg.

DWAYNE OPENED HIS EYES ON THE MORNING after his homecoming. He looked over at Donna Sue's side of the bed and saw that she was awake and in the kitchen. The couple had wrestled sexually for three bouts and now she walked into their bedroom.

She set two bedtables on the bed. One across Dwayne's lap and one for her after she got onto the bed. There was oatmeal in bowls with strawberries, toast, butter, jelly and coffee.

"Wow!" Dwayne said approvingly.

Donna Sue began buttering her toast. "Did I tell you that Benny Gordon wanted to talk to you?"

"Oh, yeah," Dwayne said. "I'll call him as soon as I eat this sumptuous, delicious and luscious breakfast. I suppose he's still working as a bouncer at the Western Danceland."

"Who knows?"

"Benny does! Ha! Ha!"

It took Dwayne a half hour to swallow all the food. When he finished he reached for the Rolodex he kept on the bedstand and looked up the Western Danceland's number. He grabbed the telephone and worked the rotary dial.

"Hello," Benny answered.

"Hi, Benny. It's me, Dwayne. What's up?"

"It's about Western Danceland. I'm now a partner with Jessie and we've had the building done over."

"Hey! That's great, pal!"

"We have the place looking snazzy and fancy. It has a very fancy western theme and the customers will dress like cowboys and cowgirls. We also have square dances on monthly evenings."

"Do you still have that screen to protect the musicians when the customers start throwing beer bottles at them."

Benny laughed. "No. We're keeping those types of customers away. You know the ones, right?"

"That would be the hillbillies, right?"

"Yeah. Me and Jessie would like for you to work for us and handle the folks that aren't dressed right. I figure we can get things in order after two or three weeks. I would work with you on that. Can you come out here this afternoon at about two o'clock? And bring Donna Sue with you. I got married. Harriet will be there so's we can introduce her to you and Donna Sue."

"Okay," Dwayne said, hanging up. He looked over at Donna Sue. "Good news, babe! Benny is now a partner with Jessie Pickens. He wants me to help him keep order in the place."

Donna Sue laughed. "Boy! That's gonna keep you busy."

"Hang on, kid. The place has been prettied up and they want to change the type of the old customers to dignified ones."

"I'll be damned!"

"Yeah! And Benny got married and he said he's gonna introduce his wife to me and you," Dwayne said. He got out from under the sheets. "He wants us there at two o'clock. And he said we'll be real surprised."

———

DWAYNE WAS DRIVING SOUTH ON HIGHWAY 81 with Donna Sue toward Western Danceland. It was a couple of miles past the Wichita city limits. Dwayne spoke seriously. "We better be careful with our conversational subjects."

"I understand," Donna Sue said, "I know that Jessie Pickens lost his wife and daughter."

"He always had trouble with those two," Dwayne said. "His wife would run off with truck drivers and then call him to come get her."

"Did he always go?"

"Yeah. I don't like to talk about his daughter."

"Then don't do it, Dwayne."

"Here's the turn off to get to Western Danceland," Dwayne said as he rolled off the cement of Highway 81 onto a macadam road. He went a quarter of a mile and saw the parking lot.

Dwayne and Donna Sue got out of their station wagon and looked at the exterior of the building. "Jesus!" Dwayne said. "I can't believe this is the Western Danceland! Look! There's been a new addition to the east side."

They walked hand-in-hand up to the door and Dwayne opened the entrance. When he and Donna Sue stepped inside both gasped. They saw the station for a maître d' then stepped into the dining area that was beautified with western art hung on the wall.

The couple heard talking to the left and walked up to a door marked **OFFICE**. Dwayne knocked on it. It was answered by Benny Gordon. He and Dwayne hugged in a manly fashion, pounding each other on the back.

"Benny!"

"Dwayne! And pretty Donna Sue! It's been a long time."

Jessie Pickens was standing with a pointer over a table that had the model of Western Danceland sitting on it. "Say hello to Donna Sue and Dwayne."

An attractive young woman was standing by Jessie. "Hi. I'm the stranger, I guess. Harriet is my name and I belong to Mister Gordon." She chuckled. "I guess that makes me Mrs. Gordon."

Both Dwayne and Donna Sue embraced her.

Jessie proudly pointed to the model. "The contractors said it will be another couple of weeks that the building and interior will be finished. But you know how them contractors are." He put the pointer off to the side. "How would you like to take a walk through the new Western Danceland?"

"Sure," Dwayne said.

"Good," Jessie said. He turned to Benny and Harriet. "Give them the tour. Okay?"

Dwayne and Benny got side by side as did Donna Sue and Harriet. They left the office and passed through a curtained entrance and stopped.

"Here's the dining room," Benny said. "I guess you saw the maître d' station, huh? That's gonna be Harriet's job."

"I couldn't resist him when he asked me to take it. He's such a handsome paratrooper."

Donna Sue said, "Dwayne's a paratrooper."

Dwayne's face reddened. "I wasn't much of a paratrooper."

Benny was curious. "Was it a military jump?"

"Uh...well, it was with the Argentine Army. On a secret operation. One jump."

Harriet looked over at Benny. "How many jumps did you make?"

"Thirty-two," Benny said. "That includes four combat jumps. I was in the Army in Europe." He looked at Dwayne. "All jumps are good jumps if you can walk away from 'em." He pointed to the tables. "You can see how they are arranged in a semi-circle in front of the orchestra. That's the dance floor to their front."

"How many tables are you going to bring in?" Dwayne asked.

"Fifty that will be arranged so that the first row is the most expensive and as the rows go back farther they get cheaper."

"When do you want me to start?"

"Tomorrow," Benny said. "There'll be a lot of work."

"I'm ready to go," Dwayne said.

"We hired an advertising company in Wichita called Prairie Publicity that's going to put announcements in both the *Eagle* and *Beacon*. We're gonna hire the KFH radio station. They'll start their presentations two weeks earlier. That will include the information that the patrons will be required to wear modern western outfits."

"Well then," Dwayne said, "we won't be eating at the Stockyard Restaurant again."

"Well," Donna Sue said, "how about going to the downtown Continental Grill now."

"That's a good idea," Harriet said. "Let's ask Jessie if he wants to come along."

"Hang on," Benny said. "I'll be right back." He walked toward the office. A half a minute later he came back. "Jessie says for us to go on. He's got some papers to go over. We can go in both automobiles since me and Harriet have to come back."

The four people headed for the door.

———

THE CONTINENTAL GRILL WAS DOWNTOWN AT 3012 Douglas. Dwayne held the door open and followed the others in. They headed down to the last booth and sat down.

A waitress came up and took everybody's order

including Dwayne's grilled cheese sandwich, French fries and Orange Crush. Benny broke out laughing. "Is that still your favorite meal?"

"Sure," Dwayne said.

The waitress returned with the ice tea for the women, coffee for Benny and Dwayne's Orange Crush. "Well!" Harriet said. "It looks like we're all going to be together for long hours."

Donna Sue took a sip of her ice tea. "Well, I won't be."

Benny stated, "I'm a partner in the business and am making you an employee-at-law, Donna Sue."

"Hey, Benny," Dwayne said. "She was a treasurer for an oil well company."

"Well, I'll be!" Benny exclaimed.

"There you go!" Dwayne said.

The waitress appeared with their lunches and everyone began eating. Benny said, "Jessie has had hard knocks what with losing his wife and daughter. He closed up for a short time, then I begged him to open. It was either that or suicide."

"Yes," Harriet said. "I sensed a good humor in him when Dwayne and Donna Sue came waltzing in."

"So did I!" Benny said. "No kidding!"

The four people ordered ice cream for dessert. Then it was time to leave. They walked out onto the sidewalk and there was handshaking and embracing.

Benny looked at Dwayne and Donna Sue. "Hey, you two! Don't be late tomorrow morning."

"Damn!" Dwayne said. "I'm gonna form a trade union!"

CHAPTER 35

O n the next day following the lunch, Dwayne and Benny pitched in with the plumbers and carpenters, putting the stoves, refrigerators, cabinets, etc. into the kitchen. When the heavier stuff was in place, the two moved into the interior of the dining room to put up the decorations that hadn't finished being put on the walls. These were such things as lariats, whips, six-guns and Indian relics. Then they turned to setting up the fifty tables.

With that done, the two guys pitched in with the workers laying out parking places for the customers' automobiles. Later strong wire fences would go around the parking area. The one thing they did not do was to work on the macadam that needed smoothed over. That they left to the tarring team.

Meanwhile, Jessie Pickens signed up a western band calling themselves *Riders Over Kansas*. The music was conducted by Fred Doolittle. Some of their songs would be *Moon Over Montana, Red River Valley, You Are My Sunshine, San Antonio Rose,* etc.

JESSIE PICKENS HAD THE PRAIRIE PUBLICITY Incorporated run advertisements in the *Wichita Eagle* and *Wichita Beacon* at an early time. The company also contacted the radio station KFH.

There was a broadcaster by the name of Harold Hopper who was a newscaster, disc jockey and special emcee. When he was given the news about the Western Danceland, he was interested. He went to the KFH manager and asked him to make a special broadcast. He got the task.

Hopper looked up in the Sedgewick County Directory and found the Western Danceland. He dialed the telephone and it was answered by a young woman.

"Hello, Miss," Hopper said. "I would like to speak to Jessie Pickens, please."

Harriet had answered the call and was sitting on the desk next to Jessie. "It's for you, Jessie."

Jessie reached for his telephone. "Hello."

"Hi, Mister Pickens. I'm Harold Hopper from KFH and I found a message on my desk about the Western Danceland."

Jessie was pleased. "Oh! How are you, Mister Hopper? What can I do for you?"

"I see that you're planning on opening a western nightclub. I'm calling to see if you would be interested in a live broadcast to present your project to the Wichita populace."

"I certainly would, Mister Hopper. I have two people I would also like to be with me."

"Ah, yes. Who might those be?"

"Well, there's my partner Benny Gordon and Dwayne Wheeler."

"The detective?"

"None other than him. He's helping Benny and me."

"Okay. And you can call me Harold."

"Fine, Harold. You can call me Jessie."

"Can you and your two men come down here tomorrow to discuss your endeavor?"

"I sure can," Jessie said. "What time?"

"How about nine o'clock in the morning?"

"That'll be fine."

Jessie hung up and turned to Harriet with a happy chuckle. "Me and the boys are gonna be on the radio!"

———

THE NEXT DAY JESSIE HAD DWAYNE AND BENNY in his Cadillac and he parked it on the curb of Market Street. They walked up to the KFH Building on William Street toward their destination. Jessie was dressed in a spangled cowboy suit complete with a "ten gallon" hat while Dwayne and Benny were dressed in suits and fedoras.

Jessie wanted them to dress like him, but Dwayne reminded him that nobody could see them going on the radio. "Wichita don't have television yet."

The trio entered the building and walked up to the counter by the elevator. A young lady typing, looked up when they approached. "Can I help you?"

"Yeah," Jessie said. "We're here to see Harold Hopper."

She looked over at a typed list of appointments. "Oh, yes. Go up on the elevator to the third floor."

"Thank you, little lady," Jessie said as a cowboy would.

"You're welcome, I'm sure," she answered, then turned back to her typewriter.

The trio had to wait for the conveyance to come down. A young kid looking like a hotel bellboy opened the door. "Going up?"

The three got in. "Third floor," Jessie said.

"Yes, sir."

The elevator reached the third floor and the kid opened the door. "Third floor," he announced.

The three got out and saw a board on the wall with names and numbers on it. They quickly found Harold Hopper's office. They walked down the hall and knocked.

"Come in," came a feminine voice.

Jessie led the way in and saw another young woman typing. She blinked at Jessie's suit for a moment, then pressed a button on an intercom. "Harold, your guests are here."

A door opened and a man wearing a shirt and an unknotted tie appeared. His trousers indicated he was a careless person since they weren't pressed.

"Come on in, guys!"

Jessie again led the way. Dwayne and Benny were close behind him. Harold closed the door. A round of hand-shaking was done and Harold went behind his desk to sit down while his three visitors each had a chair.

"Well, let's get down to business," Harold said. "So you have a western nightclub in which one must wear cowboy gear, right?"

"It sure is," Jessie said. "But this is not a hillbilly dance and whooping it up club."

"Okay," Harold acknowledged. "In other words, it will be like the Roadhouse out there on Arkansas Avenue."

Dwayne said, "It will be more Roadhouse than the

Roadhouse itself. I know the owner Elmer Pettibone and his club. As a matter of fact, I ran illegal liquor for him when I was a kid."

"I know a bit about Pettibone," Harold said. "But only *very* little!" He sat back in his chair. "What kind of music and musicians do you have?"

"These are not hillbilly, like Jessie said," Benny stated. "They travel around and now we got 'em to work with us on Friday and Saturday nights."

"Are they reliable, talented and happy in their work?

"You can say that again," Jessie said.

"What do the musicians call themselves?"

Jessie answered quickly. "*Riders Over Kansas.*"

Harold Hopper lightly rubbed his hands together for about a minute.

Dwayne, Benny and Jessie carefully watched him.

Then he stood up. "Can you be on my broadcast tonight? I want to get this out to the better half of Wichitans."

———

HAROLD HOPPER'S PROGRAM CAME ON AT 9:00 p.m. He had Dwayne, Jessie and Benny sitting with microphones on his other side. His producer Louie Burns was handling the broadcast to keep it going.

He finally showed five, four, three, two, one fingers and a fist.

Harold's voice was happy. "Good evening, Wichitans. This is Harold Hopper greeting you this week and I have something very new and very entertaining to show to you. And the man who is doing this happy-go-lucky running is Jessie Pickens. Hello, Jessie! How are you this lovely Kansas evening?"

Jessie was not afraid of microphones. "I'm fine, Harold! Fit and ready to go!"

"Why don't you tell the nice Wichitans listening in why you're in such a very happy mood."

"Certainly, Harold. A while back, I closed down my old Western Danceland. This was because of heavy sadness that had swept over me. I don't want to discuss that, Harold."

"Of course not."

"Then the Good Lord saved me and I decided to make a better Western Danceland. I called up my partner Benny Gordon with an idea I had. I told Benny that I had a hankering to rebuild a new and better Western Danceland. I told Benny that I wanted to add on to the Western Danceland by building a large restaurant where folks would get good food." He paused. "Didn't I, Benny?"

"You sure did, Jessie."

"And Benny came with a nice package to add to our operation," Jessie said. "And that was Dwayne Wheeler. And do you know what? He is that master detective that all of Wichita knows about. Say hello to the folks, Dwayne."

"Hello, folks."

"Dwayne keeps to hisself a lot unless he's out catching criminals," Jessie said. "And do you know what? Dwayne Wheeler and Benny Gordon served as U.S. Army para-troopers in the war."

Dwayne felt a stab of anger for that lie, but knew if he told the truth it would make Jessie look bad.

Now Harold Hopper jumped in. "Tell me what else you're gonna have, Jessie."

"Glad to, Harold. We're not gonna let folks in on them Friday and Saturday shindigs unless they're wearing fancy western clothing like Gene Autry, Roy Rogers or Dale Evans."

Harold spoke up. "That'll make the Western Danceland look marvelous!"

"You betcha," Jessie said. "And we're gonna have square dancing on Saturday nights once a month!"

"Well, Jessie," Gordon said. "Tell the folks how they're gonna find the Western Danceland when it's all ready to go."

"Sure thing, Harold. Go south on Highway 81 to a neon sign that's gonna be put up. It'll have an arrow on it, so just follow that."

"Thank you so very much," Harold said. "And you're gonna find me out there dancing with my wife every Saturday night including those fun square dances."

"Thank you, Harold."

Harold looked at his producer who was signaling for a series of commercials. He turned the microphones off. "Good luck, Jessie."

CHAPTER 36

The brand new Western Danceland opened only five weeks later. On that first Friday, the cars started showing up at five-thirty p.m. The announcements in the *Wichita Eagle* and *Wichita Beacon* that the doors would open at six o'clock p.m. was greeted with the customers hurrying to have some cowboy fun.

Dwayne, Jessie, Benny, Donna Sue and Harriet were standing at the front door watching the newcomers. Jessie could only stand it for ten minutes. "Dwayne, you and Benny go over to the gate and tell the gatekeepers Larson and Gaddis to let those folks drive inside the fence right now."

Dwayne and Benny went through the restaurant. They noticed the *Riders Over Kansas* musicians were just starting to warm up under their band leader Fred Doolittle.

"Get ready!" Benny shouted to them as he and Dwayne passed by.

There were two gatekeepers who saw Dwayne and

Benny hurrying up to them. "Okay, guys," Dwayne said. "Open the gate!"

"And make sure the folks in the cars are wearing western gear," Benny added.

Gaddis and Larson opened the gates and signaled to the customers to start driving in. The two inspected the cars to make sure they were cowboys and cowgirls. Meanwhile, Jessie sent Harriet to get to the maître d' position.

As the line of people getting out of their cars were going through the front door to Harriet's station she could only handle ten parties at a time.

The customers who had to wait were in a good humor, laughing and looking around at the decorations. Jessie walked down the line that stood outside and did his best to keep them in good humor. They were laughing with him in their cowboy and cowgirl outfits.

"Hey!" Jessie spoke loudly. "You folks just wait and see what goodies you're gonna have inside there!"

"Do you have a rodeo?" one cowboy asked laughing.

"No," somebody else called out. "We're gonna see who can herd cows the best."

"I bet we can see Wyatt Earp!"

"Are bucking wild horses in there?" another jovial cowboy said. "That's what I want to see!"

A trio of cowboys and cowgirls began singing *She'll Be Coming Around the Mountain!* A moment later others joined in with them.

Dwayne and Benny were keeping a sharp eye on the people outdoors to make sure all were dressed western. "Y'know, Benny," Dwayne said. "I've figured out these folks. They're not hillbillies and not filthy rich."

"What are they then?" Benny asked.

"They're smart people," Dwayne answered. "They're

carpenters, printers, plumbers, and automobile mechanics. Workers like that."

"Yeah," Benny said. "You won't find them in Elmer Pettibone's Roadhouse or the Prairie Wind Golf and Tennis Club out there in Eastborough."

Inside the Western Danceland, the crowd was steadily getting larger.

———

IT WAS TWO O'CLOCK IN THE MORNING WHEN the last of the cowboys and cowgirls drove out of the parking lot and turned north for Wichita. All the clean-up in the kitchen, dining, and restrooms was over with. Fred Doolittle and his musicians were also gone.

In Jessie's office he grinned as Donna Sue counted the take for the evening. When she finished adding everything, she sighed. "Whew!"

"What'd we get?" Jessie asked.

"Eight hundred dollars," she answered. "That's above our cost of salaries, food, beverages and a few other things."

Dwayne lit a Lucky Strike. "Donna Sue knows her finances. She worked on an oil company's funds a couple of years ago. And then there's also our agency."

"Well!" Jessie said. "We have another go at it tomorrow. So ever'body go home and rest up."

———

THE SECOND NIGHT WAS EVEN BETTER THAN THE first. Wichitans liked going out on Saturdays or Fridays. There were also some folks that came back for a second time.

The employees worked faster and more efficiently. Jessie put an upturned Stetson on the dais of Fred Doolittle's *Riders Over Kansas* for the dancers to drop money in. The waiters were also getting better tips as were Vince Larson and Roy Gaddis the gatekeepers.

There was a couple of intoxicated cowboys but their wives took care of them and paid the gatekeepers to take them out to their cars.

At the end of the evening, Donna Sue counted out $1,054.

———

THE NEXT COMING WEEK WAS MADE UP OF Sunday, Monday and Tuesday being taken off. The preparation work was Wednesday and Thursday. Then it was Friday and Saturday to be back in for the entertainment.

The two ladies, Donna Sue and Harriet, kept their eyes on the office doing paperwork and answering the telephones for people that wanted reservations. Dwayne and Benny kept order in both the interior and exterior of the action.

Fred Doolittle's band was getting loud applause at the end of their songs. One Wichitan cowboy thanked Fred by saying, "You made this a real nice evening."

"You sure did, honey," his slightly tipsy wife said.

Outside, things were going along excellently. The cars were coming in courteous and the gatekeepers had no problem. Then a Model A automobile drove up. There were four people in the car. Two men in front and two women in the rear.

Roy Gaddis, the gatekeeper, said, "Sir, you can't go into the parking lot."

"Whattaya mean we cain't go into the parking lot."

"You're not in cowboy apparel," Gaddis said.

"Oh, yeah?" The guy got out of the car. "Looky here. I got on a cowboy suit." He was wearing bib overalls over a woolen checkered shirt. He also wore army boots and a soiled baseball cap.

"That's not a cowboy costume," Gaddis added.

Vince Larson walked up. "What's the trouble?"

"This guy says he's looking like a cowboy," Roy said.

At that point the guy's partner got out of their car. "Looky hyar at me. I look as much a cowboy as my pal is."

Roy glared at him. "You're not coming in the parking lot or the Western Danceland."

At that point, Dwayne walked into the picture. "What's up?"

Vince said, "These two guys say they got cowboy stuff on."

Dwayne laughed. "That don't look cowboy."

The women in the back seat were embarrassed. That encouraged the two men to defend their appearances. "What's not cowboy about the way we're dressed?"

The other man in the Model A spoke up angrily. "We used to be able to go in there when Jessie ran it!"

Dwayne was understanding in what he just heard. "Well, listen up now. Ol' Jessie would be real glad to see you, but he's changed things. And I can tell you honestly that if you came back wearing cowboy stuff you and your missus would be most welcomed"

"Well," the man said. "How much does that cowboy stuff cost?"

"There's a boot store downtown," Dwayne said. "They can sell you about everything you'd need."

"Okay, I guess."

"By the way," Dwayne said. "There's not a strong wire in front of the orchestra like it was in the old days. So you wouldn't be able to throw beer bottles at the musicians."

The men got back into the Model A and the driver got out of the line and drove off the property.

As the weeks rolled by, more of the old customers had to be turned away. Dwayne Wheeler, Benny Gordon and the gatekeepers felt sorry for them. Not a one had the enough money to dress up like a cowboy. Jessie was the sorriest about the situation, but he had to keep his scenario alive.

CHAPTER 37

It was Tuesday, a day off from the Western Danceland, and Donna Sue left the apartment to go downstairs where the mailboxes were located. There was only one letter that was in a stiff envelope. It was addressed to:

Mr. and Mrs. Dwayne Wheeler.

She carried it upstairs and into the apartment. "We got a letter. You want to look at it?"

Dwayne was reading the sports page of the *Wichita Eagle*. "Nope."

Donna Sue opened it up and pulled out the card. "Oh! It's from Terry McCarthy. He and Lois Chapman are getting married at the Prairie Wind Golf and Tennis Club in Eastborough."

"Where else?" Dwayne said. "They'll be dressed up high and mighty."

"They want us to attend."

"What's the day and date?"

"It's Monday next week at two o'clock in the afternoon."

Dwayne looked at the newspaper and saw the date. "Yeah. The day and date are right for us."

"Mmm!" Donna Sue said. "It looks like it might have been mailed kind of late."

Dwayne chuckled. "Yeah! Terry prob'ly had to drop to his knees and beg the Chapman family to invite a private detective and his wife."

"Well, they didn't mention any registered things for us to get."

"Great!" Dwayne said. "Let's get Terry a carton of Pall Mall cigarettes."

"The register is more for the bride."

"Okay then. Get her a brassiere and some panties."

"Dwayne! Get serious!"

Dwayne shuddered. "Okay. Go to Rorabaugh's Department Store then."

"Listen, wise guy," Donna Sue said. "You're gonna drive me down there and stay with me. It's located at Broadway and Douglas, remember?"

"Okay," Dwayne growled.

They dressed for shopping and walked over to the E.Z. Parking Garage to get their station wagon. "Listen," Donna Sue said, "don't start complaining. It takes a while to get a wedding gift."

Dwayne drove over to the Rorabaugh and found an empty place on the curb to park. Donna Sue led the way into the store. She found a floorwalker and asked him where the marriage department was. He told her the way and Dwayne followed her.

A well-dressed young lady behind a counter spoke to them. "Can I help you?"

Donna Sue began talking with the expert on wedding

gifts. One and one-half hour passed by and finally Donna Sue called Dwayne over to show him what she had purchased.

"Looky, Dwayne! This is real nice. It's a tea set."

Dwayne grudgingly looked at the water kettle, serving tray, creamer, sugar bowl, and teapot. "What's the cost?"

"Don't worry about the cost, sweetie," Donna Sue said. "You can always get money by taking one of those horrible machine guns in the door jamb to pay for it."

"Well," Dwayne said, "that's not a good idea. Let's pay for it. Those swells from Eastborough will be impressed."

"Oh! You're such a good boy, Dwayne!"

———

ON THE WEDDING DAY, DWAYNE AND DONNA SUE showed up at the Prairie Wind Golf and Tennis Club right on time. Dwayne was dressed in his fedora and suit while Donna Sue wore a French plume-genre hat and a formaliste modele dress. As they walked into the hall, Dwayne gave his hat to the woman in the hat booth. After that a young boy took Donna Sue's boxed gift to the ballroom.

Dwayne and Donna Sue entered matrimonial hall that was crowded with people unknown to either one of them. They picked out a pew and slid into it. A shadow came across the couple, and Dwayne looked up.

Terry McCarthy patted his shoulder. "I'm real happy to see that you and your lady accepted the wedding invitation."

"Who's your wife's father?" Donna Sue asked.

"Dan Chapman," Terry answered. "He's one of the vice presidents at Boeing."

The hall kept filling up and Terry said, "I got to go up

to the alter to join my best man. It's Carl Banter, the attorney." He was a friend to both Dwayne and Terry.

Terry and Carl sat down on the front pew to wait for the ceremony to begin. Fifteen minutes passed until anything happened.

The parson, a man who was a pastor of the Chapman family in the Methodist Church of Eastborough, now came out. He nodded to the organ player and the lady started up the *Wedding March*.

Terry and Carl looked up to see Dan Chapman escorting his daughter down to be given away. Everybody's heads turned to watch the procession. Lois stepped away from her father when they reached the alter. Terry took her arm.

The pastor began reciting the service. When he reached the end, Terry put the wedding ring on Lois' finger and kissed her. The couple turned to go back up the aisle. Everybody went ahead of them and when the newlyweds came out the door the rice flew.

The husband and bride went around to the ballroom and the congregation followed. There were nameplates on the tables and Dwayne and Donna Sue found theirs in the back.

"Well," Dwayne said. "I guess that shows our ranking, huh?" He looked over at Donna Sue and saw she was crying.

"This is so beautiful," she said.

"Good God!" Dwayne hissed. "If it wasn't for Terry we wouldn't be here at all."

The wedding cake was wheeled out and everyone left their chairs to watch the happy couple cut into it. Dwayne and Donna Sue joined the throng to watch the ceremony. The bride and groom kept the first cut, then the saucers were wheeled up so the congregation could get their pieces of the pastry.

Thirty minutes later the repast was passed out. There were eight waiters and waitresses doing the job and no one took a bite until everyone else was served.

Dwayne and Donna Sue were seated at the last table to be served. When the dinner was finished, the same waiters and waitresses cleared off the tables. Dwayne and Donna Sue sat where the last to be taken away.

The orchestra entered and when they were set up, they began to play a Strauss Waltz so that the father of the bride could dance with his daughter. Then the second song was played and Terry danced with her. When that ceremonial music was finished, the next songs were up-to-date.

Donna Sue pulled Dwayne onto the dance floor. They did three dances in a row, then went back to their table. Five minutes later Carl Banter walked up. "Hey there, Donna Sue and Dwayne. What are you doing way back here?"

The other diners at the table looked at him with frowns. Dwayne shrugged.

"My God!" Carl exclaimed. "You're Dwayne Wheeler the detective."

Now everyone at the table looked over at him. One man burst out laughing. "There's a brave hero here and we're sitting with him. We're only managers and supervisors at Boeing. All these tables close around here are the same like we are."

Dwayne looked at him. "Y'know, pal, there ain't nothing wrong with you guys."

Donna Sue smiled. "I worked at Boeing as a welder during the war and then got to be a supervisor. And I'm this brave guy's wife!"

The people around the table clapped and the next three tables looked over to see what was happening. Suddenly Dwayne Wheeler's presence was known. Little by little the news passed around the room. The executives living in Eastborough were finally reached and they joined in admiring the shamus.

The bride's mother Lucille Chapman was not happy with what was going on. Her husband Vice President Dan Chapman had made her send out invitations to the managers and supervisors of Boeing after an argument with her.

Dwayne stood up and smiled. He took his glass and raised it, saying, "God bless our married couple."

Now clapping and whistling crossed the entire ballroom.

CHAPTER 38

Before Dwayne Wheeler had left the Prairie Wind Golf and Tennis Club he found out that several of the Boeing managers and supervisors were going to the Western Danceland for their Friday and/or Saturday fun.

However, the appearance of "hillbillies" was increasing. Some feelings were hurt when they were turned back. There were very few physical attacks on the gatekeepers Larson and Gaddis. However, on one occasion Dwayne and Benny Gordon had to help out the gatekeepers.

They ended up calling the Highway Patrol to arrest a particularly tough little guy. His wife, who was larger than him, stayed in their car that was an old Ford Coupé. Her husband was wrestled to the ground and handcuffed. The Highway Patrolman put him inside the patrol car. The diminutive man struggled then gave it up.

He looked out the window and shrieked at Dwayne and Benny. "My name is Howard Linking! You better remember that. Howard Linking! I'm coming back and blowing your God damn heads off!"

Mrs. Linking, who was embarrassed, went one way and the Highway Patrolman with Linking went the other.

———

THE PHONE RANG IN THE WHEELER APARTMENT and Dwayne picked it up since Donna Sue was in the shower. It was Terry McCarthy. "Hi, Dwayne."

"Hi, Terry. How does it feel to be a married man?

"Pretty good. I called you because Jim Ferguson wants to talk to you."

"Really?"

"Yeah. I don't know what it's all about but I'm guessing it's something you might have done."

"He's an F.B.I. hotshot," Dwayne said. "What would he want from me?"

"I don't know. But he's here in Wichita and wants you to answer a few questions. He's staying at the Riverview Hotel. He doesn't know I'm making this call, but I thought I'd warn you."

"Well, thanks, Terry."

Dwayne hung up just as Donna Sue walked out of the bathroom wearing her robe. "Who was that?"

"It was Terry McCarthy. He called me to be on my toes."

"Ha! Are you gonna be a ballet dancer?"

"Don't laugh, baby," Dwayne said, irritated. "A very high-up in the F.B.I. wants to ask me a few questions."

"Oh, Dwayne! It's those damn machine guns in the doorjambs."

Dwayne stood up. "I got to do some scouting." He picked up the phone and dialed the Riverview Hotel where the F.B.I. was staying.

He was acquainted with the house detective, who was

retired from the Wichita Police Department. "Hi, Harry... fine...Can you get loose...good. Meet me at the corner of Douglas and Seneca at the Dockum Drug Store in about fifteen minutes." He got his fedora, keys and wallet and trotted over to the E.Z. Parking Garage.

Dwayne drove on Seneca and saw Harry Denver, who was the retired Wichita policeman now the house detective at the Riverside Hotel. He honked his horn at him and saw him come over.

They both walked into the Dockum Drug Store and went to the fountain area. The waitress came up and Dwayne ordered an ice cream sundae and Harry did the same. When she came back with the refreshments, Harry took a bite then asked, "What's up?"

"You got an F.B.I. guy in the hotel, right?"

"Yeah. He's on the second floor and his two men are on the third."

"Has he talked to anybody?"

"Yeah. There was a local F.B.I. that visited him."

"Yeah," Dwayne said. "He was Terry McCarthy."

"That's the guy," Harry said, then dipped his spoon in the sundae. "D'you have a problem, Dwayne?"

"Yeah," Dwayne said. "I got a call from Terry."

"Do you want me to check out this Terry?" Harry asked.

"No," Dwayne said. "We were together on an operation but it's gonna be me the F.B.I. was interested in." He slid off the stool. "Thanks, Harry."

"Okay. I'm gonna get another sundae."

Dwayne hurried for the door.

When he drove into the parking garage, the shamus jogged over to their apartment. He burst in and startled Donna Sue who was reading the *Ladies Home Journal*.

"What in the world!" she cried out.

"We got trouble," Dwayne said. "I talked with Harry Denver the house dick. He said there's three F.B.I. agents in the Riverview Hotel. And he's sure they're looking for me."

"When will they come here?"

"I wish I knew," Dwayne said. "But I'm going to tighten up that door jamb. And don't you look at it while they're here."

"Oh, those God damned submachine guns," Donna Sue wailed.

"Not *submachine guns* they're *Tommy guns!*"

——————

IT WAS EARLY IN THE MORNING THAT TWO F.B.I. agents knocked on the door of the Wheeler apartment. The door opened and Dwayne was in his bathrobe holding a copy of the *Wichita Eagle* when he opened it.

"Yeah?"

Three agents showed their I.D. and Federal search identification. "Am I speaking to Dwayne Wheeler?"

"Yeah?"

"Hello, Dwayne," Jim Ferguson said.

"Hi, Jim. How's things?"

"Tell me. Are you in possession of two Tommy guns?"

Dwayne smirked. "Why? Have you lost a couple?"

"This is serious," Ferguson inquired.

"Well, I can tell you truthful that I'm not even near any Tommy guns," Dwayne said. "The only firearm I got is a .45 caliber automatic pistol. I am a licensed private detective."

Donna Sue walked in from the bedroom looking nonchalant in her housedress. "Oh! We have visitors."

"These three guys are F.B.I. agents," Dwayne said. "They want to know if we have Tommy guns."

"What!" Donna Sue said. "Tommy who has guns?"

"This is serious," Ferguson said. He glared at Dwayne. "Do you recall driving an armored truck full of cigarettes?"

"Okay," Dwayne said. "Now I know what you're after. It was at night and we were on a very rough road. We came over the hump on the road and received automatic fire. I was with my partner driver name of Jerry Owens. We both had to move fast and we opened the doors and fired back. We killed three young guys. They had Tommy guns."

"All right," Ferguson said. "Go ahead."

"Well, the authorities showed up. They got down from our truck and walked over to the dead guys. There were cars behind them and they saw footprints and started out to find the owners."

"Then what did you do?"

"We knew our cargo wasn't worth much by then," Dwayne said. "So Jerry and I backed up and went up a few miles to the highway and drove back to Wichita."

Jim Ferguson stated, "I'm afraid we're going to have to search your house, Mrs. Wheeler."

He showed her his F.B.I. identification and Federal rights to search their home. "If you'll excuse us, we'll get to our duties."

Donna Sue showed annoyance. "I resent that! Those Treasury guys have already done that!"

"Why don't you sit down on your sofa and let us do our job," Jim Ferguson asked.

"Do you guys want a beer?" Dwayne asked. "I got some in the refrigerator."

Ferguson and the other agents thanked him and the three got to work.

They went into the kitchen and began opening and closing things, making noises. With that done, both went through the furniture in the living room. They made Dwayne and Donna Sue stand up and watch.

The next step was going into the bedroom. They made a mess of the two closets, a bed, a throw rug, chest of drawers and a dresser. The bathroom was given a clean surveillance.

They walked back into the living room. "We want you to stay in Wichita."

"Well, we work at a place called the Western Danceland," Dwayne said. "It's just south on Highway 81. Drop in but you have to be wearing cowboy outfits."

"Sorry," Jim Ferguson said. "I left my ten gallon hat and spurs back in Washington."

CHAPTER 39

It turned out the F.B.I. had gotten nowhere in Wichita, Kansas. Terry McCarthy called up Dwayne and told him they had already left the Riverview Hotel and headed out to the Wichita Municipal Airport.

"Where are they going?"

"It's hard to tell since Jim Ferguson is in charge," Terry said. "I'll bet they were headed to Boston. He probably told his two guys to tear up Franklin Ward and Jefferson Ward to find those Tommy guns. Maybe there's some hidden Insurance Men that we missed."

"Yeah," Dwayne said. "Maybe they'll find a whole lot of them in a secret Mafia family. Ferguson is probably gonna run ex-Lieutenant Gerald Harrigan through the wringer."

"I'll bet Salvatore Sica is gonna get a citation," Terry said. "He did an excellent job."

"He sure as hell will."

"I forgot to thank you for the tea set," Terry said. "Lois hasn't gotten around to writing the thank-you notes."

"I'll tell Donna Sue."

———

Jessie Pickens had to purchase ten more tables and forty chairs. He had been smart to leave room for more furniture during construction. He called in Dwayne and Benny to lend a hand even though he had hired two janitors.

The janitors did sweeping and mopping while Dwayne and Benny waited for the delivery from Wards Furniture. They stood out front waiting for the arrival of the goods. Jessie saved more money by letting Dwayne and Benny unload the deliveries and bring them into the building.

"It seems the gatekeepers should do this," Benny grouched.

"Yeah," Dwayne said. "And this is one of our days off."

Fifty minutes went by when they heard the engine of the delivery truck. When it came into sight, Benny signaled it to back up to the front door.

The truck driver did as he was told. He stopped and hopped out of the cab. "Howdy, guys. I'm told you'll take these things in yourselves."

"That's right," Dwayne said.

The trucker opened his back doors and adjusted a ramp to slide things on. "Okay. Have at it."

Dwayne and Benny started with the tables. They grabbed the first table and maneuvered it down the ramp. It was carried in where Jessie was waiting.

"Put that one over there," he said.

His two employees did as they were told.

This was repeated nine times more.

"Okay, fellers," Jessie said. "There's forty chairs in there that are just crying to be lugged inside."

Dwayne and Benny carried two chairs each down the ramp. Jessie had them put under the tables just right. All in all, the two workers brought in forty chairs and arranged them the way Jessie wanted them.

The unloading was completed and the truck drove away. Dwayne and Benny watched the driver disappear in a cloud of dust. Jessie gave them orders for the next job. "Put on the tablecloths."

They did the chore with Jessie looking on at his two employees. The boss made sure there was no wrinkles in the tablecloths.

Dwayne looked at Jessie and sneered. "Do you want us to dig a moat around the building?"

Jessie laughed. "You guys are really funny."

————

FRIDAY EVENING WAS TIME FOR EVERYONE TO make sure things were in order. Dwayne and Benny put their .45 automatic pistols in their office closet. After getting ready in their cowboy attire, the pair went out to make sure the gatekeepers were in good shape as they directed the parking.

When enough people were inside, Dwayne and Benny split to keep on different sides of the dining room and ballroom. Dwayne walked slowly, smiling and nodding.

A man who was a supervisor at Boeing looked at him and gave a whoop. "There you are! We saw you at the McCarthy wedding."

Dwayne gave him a big grin. "Yeah! You were at the table next to mine. How's things going?"

"Just fine," the supervisor said.

Dwayne drifted among other people whom he recognized from past times. "Enjoying yourselves, I see," he said.

"You bet, Dwayne!"

The band leader Fred Doolittle brought out his musicians to sit down and tune their instruments. There was scattered clapping to show the appreciation to the music makers.

Now the waiters came out. Some were moving to show menus while others went through the maître d' Harriet who sent the customers inside the ropes that were very close to the dancing area.

At that time, Dwayne went to the office to relax a bit. Donna Sue was getting ready to start adding up the tickets. She didn't like having to do that sort of arithmetic all at once. She looked across her desk at Dwayne. "How are things going?"

"Okay. I've run into a couple of people who were at the wedding. Boeing folks."

Benny Gordon sauntered in. "Hi."

Out on the band, Fred Doolittle started his musical program with *You Are My Sunshine.*

Most of the crowd got up and went out onto the dance floor.

Jessie came in from greeting people and was having a lot of fun. He sat down on the couch. "Hey! Y'know what? We ought to get a comedian."

"Good idea," Dwayne said. "But where are you going to get one?"

"That's the trouble in Wichita," Jessie said. "The only comics we can get are on the radio. Remember vaudeville? We could get funny folks in those days."

Benny shrugged. "All them vaudeville people are on

the radio now. Jack Benny, Fred Allen, Jimmy Durante, Sophie Tucker and all the rest."

Dwayne stood up. "C'mon, Benny. Let's go and check out the gatekeepers."

"Okay, pal."

They walked through the club house and outside. The gatekeepers were taking it easy. Vince Larson, sitting on a stool, stretched. "Those ten tables came in handy."

His pal Roy Gaddis nodded.

As the four men took it easy, an ancient Ford Coupé came past the gate and stopped at the front door. Howard Linking, the angry hillbilly, was driving and he had a Henry Rifle 15-sh0t lever action repeating rifle .44 rim-fire. He had a haversack over his shoulder that was filled with loose bullets. He reached over and picked up the long gun.

"Alright, you God damn swells!"

Linking jumped out of the coupé and rushed through the door past a shocked Harriet Gordon. He burst into the dining area and started shooting up in the air.

"Kiss my ass!" he shouted.

Out where the gatekeepers were sitting Dwayne and Benny ran around to where the rifle was being fired. The pair got their .45 automatic pistols from the closets and hurried out to see who was yelling and shooting.

Dwayne and Benny saw that Linking was shooting straight up toward the ceiling while the audience was charging through the door leading out to the gatekeepers who were standing there stupefied as the crowd ran past and around them.

Howard Linking was loading the rifle with his eyes away from Dwayne and Benny. "His rifle is empty!" Dwayne said. "Shoot for his legs!"

He and Benny shot the hillbilly in the knees. He went

down and the two pistoleros ran over and kicked his rifle away. Donna Sue and Harriet walked in, noting all was safe.

Linking was breathing hard.

Vince Larson and Roy Gaddis tiptoed in and breathed a sigh of relief to see that the interior was not damaged. The band sat in their chairs without having moved.

Larson and Gaddis ran outside and announced that the shooter was down and unconscious.

Now Jessie came running in and he noted that the only place that was shot up was the ceiling. He went in the office and called the Kansas Highway Patrol.

Dwayne and Benny went back to see that Linking was going into shock. The pair took off their belts and put one around each of Linking's legs. There was still fight in him. He gazed at Dwayne and Benny. He sneered, "I reckon I skeered y'all, hey?"

"I reckon you did," Dwayne said. "I'm just happy you're a lousy shot."

"Yeah," Benny spoke.

"I ain't no lousy shot!" Linking growled. "I din't want to kill nobody. They'd hang me in Leavenworth."

"I guess they would," Dwayne said.

Linking raised his right hand and point out. "Ha! Look at them bullet holes up there."

Dwayne looked at the man for a couple of minutes. "Where's your wife?"

"Daisy's at home," Linking said. "She's proud of me."

The sound of sirens could be heard as the ambulance and a patrol car arrived.

CHAPTER 40

Judge William Dodge was getting ready to try Howard Linking in the Sedgwick County Court. He was an impatient man and he entered the courtroom frowning. After glancing around he took a deep breath and looked over at his bench, then sat down.

The Judge had looked at a little man by the name of Howard Linking who was clad in his jail coveralls. He was in a wheelchair next to his lawyer Carl Banter. Both were seated at the defendant's table. Daisy Linking was sitting behind her husband in the spectator part of the court.

The plaintiff's table was occupied by District Attorney Wyatt Cunningham with his young Deputy District Attorney Mary Miller. Judge Dodge turned his attention to the jury that had already been taken care of. They were seven men, five women and three men as extras.

His Honor nodded to the bailiff. That was the signal for Bailiff Donald Jones to speak. "All rise. The Sedgwick Court is now in session, the Judge William Dodge preceding. Be seated. The trial is called to order. District

Attorney Wyatt Cunningham called Jessie Pickens to the bench."

The bailiff Jones spoke. "Raise your right hand. Do you solemnly affirm that the testimony you are about to give will faithfully and truthfully conform to the facts and rules of the court?"

"I do," Jessie said.

"You may take a seat."

The District Attorney Wyatt Cunningham spoke. "State your name, please."

"I'm Jessie Pickens."

"What is your profession, Mister Pickens?"

"I own a nightclub called the Western Danceland."

"Is the nightclub located in Sedgwick County?" Mister Pickens asked.

"It is, sir."

"Did your nightclub suffer rifle fire six weeks ago?"

"Yes, sir."

"Is the person who fired that rifle in this courtroom, Mister Pickens? And will you point him out if he is present."

"Yes, sir." He pointed to Howard Linking seated in a wheelchair.

"Let the record show that Howard Linking is seated in a wheelchair. Was anyone injured or killed, Mister Pickens?"

"Only Mister Linking."

"Was there any damage caused by Mister Linking?"

"Yes. He shot the ceiling into pieces. It will be very expensive to repair."

"What about the people who enjoyed entertainment in the Western Danceland, Mister Pickens. Were any injured?"

"There were none injured but they certainly did not enjoy having somebody shooting over their heads."

"You may step down, Mister Pickens."

Judge Dodge looked over at Banter and asked, "Do you wish to interrogate Mister Pickens?"

"No," Banter said.

"I wish to call Mister Dwayne Wheeler," Wyatt Cunningham stated.

The bailiff spoke out. "Call Mister Dwayne Wheeler."

Dwayne was called in from the hall. He was sworn in and invited to sit down.

District Attorney Wyatt Cunningham asked, "What is your profession, Mister Wheeler?"

"I am a private detective working in the Western Danceland," Dwayne said.

"Are you aware of somebody firing a rifle into the ceiling?"

"Yes, I was there when the incident took place."

"What steps did you take, Mister Wheeler?"

Dwayne pointed at Howard Linking. "We shot him in his legs then put tourniquets on his knees when we saw he was no longer a danger to us."

"That is all I have," Cunningham said.

Judge Dodge asked Banter, "Do you wish to interrogate Mister Wheeler?"

"No," Banter said standing up. "I'm not going to speak to my client. I am going to tell everybody here who Mister Howard Linking really is." He crossed his arms over his chest. "And I would like it to include Dwayne Wheeler."

Judge Dodge looked at the District Attorney. "Do you have any objection, Mister Cunningham?"

The District Attorney shrugged. "No objection."

Judge Dodge turned to Carl Banter. "You may proceed, Mister Banter."

"Thank you, Your Honor," Carl Banter said. He cleared his throat. "Howard Linking is in his mid-forties. He came to Wichita to work in the Boeing Airplane Company at the start of World War Two. He was hired as a sheet metal worker since he was not able to read well. His Texas family were only sharecroppers and not able to keep him in school. He was proud of his job at Boeing and was able to stay on after the war was over."

Wyatt Cunningham stood up. "I object. This has nothing to do with the Western Danceland."

Carl Banter replied, "It has everything to do about the Western Danceland and what happened that evening."

Judge Dodge said, "Objection overruled."

Banter continued. "Howard Linking was proud of his life at Boeing. He has a wife by the name of Daisy that also came from a Texas sharecropper's family and she is proud of their married life. She is seated in the spectator area behind him." He paused then spoke again. "I would like Dwayne Wheeler recalled to the stand, Your Honor."

"So be it," the Judge said. "Mister Wheeler is already sworn in."

Dwayne was seated in the spectator area. He got up and walked up to the witness chair. He was confused about what Carl Banter was going to do.

"Hello, Dwayne," Banter said. "We're well acquainted, are we not?"

"We sure are, Carl."

"Okay then. Were you surprised when you came upon Mister Linking shooting at the ceiling?"

"Well, yeah. At first I thought there was going to be blood all over the room. But I noticed that Mister Linking was firing only into the ceiling. My partner Benny Gordon was also surprised."

Banter asked, "You and Mister Gordon fired together into his legs. Why did you do that?"

"We had dealt with Mister Linking before and figured he would lower his weapon and start shooting at people. Those people were bunched together around the door in order to escape."

"Did he reload his firearm, Dwayne?"

"No. When he shot all his ammunition in his rifle, he pointed at the ceiling and laughed. Even after we shot his legs. Then he looked at me and Benny and bragged about the number of bullets he had shot. And he said Daisy was at home and was proud. Daisy is his wife sitting behind him."

Banter turned to Judge Dodge. "Your Honor, I believe that Howard Linking and his physical and mental reactions show that he is unable to be logical. I spoke with Mrs. Linking three times and on the third she broke down and said her husband Howard was not rational. And he was also able to endure pain."

Judge Dodge nodded his head to Carl Banter. "I am going to turn your client in for psychiatric analysis." He looked over at District Attorney Wyatt Cunningham. "It appears the prisoner will be taken out of the Sedgwick County Jail and turned over to the Saint Michael Hospital here in Wichita."

"Very well, Your Honor."

The Judge stood up and banged his gavel. "Court dismissed."

CHAPTER 41

Dwayne Wheeler made up his mind to go back being a private detective after the trial. Donna Sue was happy with his decision. It was on a rainy day when the pair went to their office on Harry Street.

Donna Sue called Millie at the Reliable Answering Service. When the operator answered she squealed with delight. "Are you working again, Donna Sue?"

"We sure are."

"You missed lots of callers while you were gone," Millie told her. "I stacked up so many slips of paper that my boss told me to throw them away."

"Well, you can count on us now," Donna Sue said.

Donna Sue had gotten Daisy Linking a place to work at the Whitaker Laundry in downtown Wichita. She had done this long before when Maybelle Gilhooly was having a hard time. Donna Sue also got Mrs. Linking a room at the Randall Hotel like she did for Maybelle.

Now Dwayne had got his office area cleaned up at about the same time Donna Sue had gotten all her paperwork finished. They had both taken fifteen hours doing it.

Dwayne had an idea. "Let's get supper at the Continental Grill on Market Street."

"Yeah," Donna Sue said. "I can use that wonderful restaurant." She paused. "What are you gonna have?"

"Let me see," Dwayne said. "How about if I order a grilled cheese sandwich, French fries and I'll wash it down with Orange Crush."

"I should have known,' Donna Sue said. "C'mon let's get over to Market Street."

————

DWAYNE AND DONNE SUE ENTERED THEIR apartment after eating at the Continental Grill. The couple was tired but happy as they walked to the window and looked out over the city.

"You know what, Donna Sue?"

"No."

"I like Wichita, Kansas."

"Mmm, me, too."

A grin appeared on Dwayne's face. "And I've got a feeling that a new caper is right about the corner!"

A Look At Book 7:

Wichita Snatched

1950s Wichita, Kansas

Private Detective Dwayne Wheeler and his wife Donna Sue take on their latest case investigating the disappearance of five innocent girls who were promised stardom but instead found themselves trapped in a human trafficking ring.

As they embark on a high-stakes investigation that takes them on a snipe hunt through Hollywood and beyond—chasing leads and following clues—Dwayne and Donna never lose sight of their mission to bring the missing girls home safely, even as they're mistaken for aspiring stars by producers.

The dynamic duo must work together to uncover the truth and solve the mystery before it's too late. But will their escapades lead them down the right path and bring the girls to safety?

Wichita Payback is book seven in a historical private eye series that follows Dwayne Wheeler—a tough and hardboiled detective.

AVAILABLE JULY 2023

About the Author

Patrick Andrews was born an Army Brat on January 14, 1936—his sister's arrival just two years later. His father was a paratrooper in the 82nd Airborne Division during World War II. His mother was a good army officer's wife, who, like several of her lady cousins, wrote short-stories and poems.

After the war, Patrick's father transferred into the Army Reserves, and they moved to Wichita, Kansas—where Patrick caught the scribbling bug. When Patrick got a job as a copy boy at the *Wichita Eagle* newspaper, he was ecstatic.

A few years later, Patrick got a yen to be a paratrooper. He enlisted in the Army and took basic training in Camp Chaffee, Arkansas, soon after being transferred to the 82nd Airborne Division in Fort Bragg. His career with the 82nd was rewarding—being promoted to sergeant and tasked with training cadets in West Point before retiring.

When Patrick read James Jones' *From Here to Eternity*, he appreciated the pride and struggling of soldiers. Soon after, he moved to San Diego, California and began writing and mailing manuscripts while working at a union typesetting company. He married and had one child, named William Patrick.

One pivotal night, Patrick was with a couple of his writing buddies, drinking scotch whiskey and playing at writing the *Sixgun Samurai* series. The next day, they drove up to Pinnacle Books in Los Angeles, where they walked out with a book deal. Patrick and his friends went on to write the series' twelve novels—which were also printed in the U.K. by Star Books, the paperback division of W.H. Allen & Co.

From then on, Patrick started writing and selling western, men's adventure, and military fiction. Years passed, and he had 24 published e-books with Piccadilly Publishing in the U.K.

Today, all six of Patrick's Wichita Detective books are getting another chance to see the light of day—with Rough Edges Press—and find refuge on a cozy shelf in Ocean Hills, California where Patrick and his beloved wife, Julie, live.